SkyRoom

LARRY GAUDET

For Alison and our sons, Jackson and Theo

You take delight not in a city's seven or seventy wonders,
but in the answer it gives to a question of yours.

—Italo Calvino, *Invisible Cities*

TABLE OF CONTENTS

1
Procession

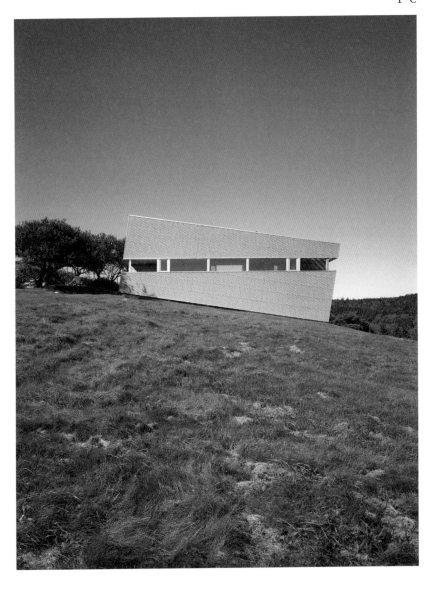

I-E

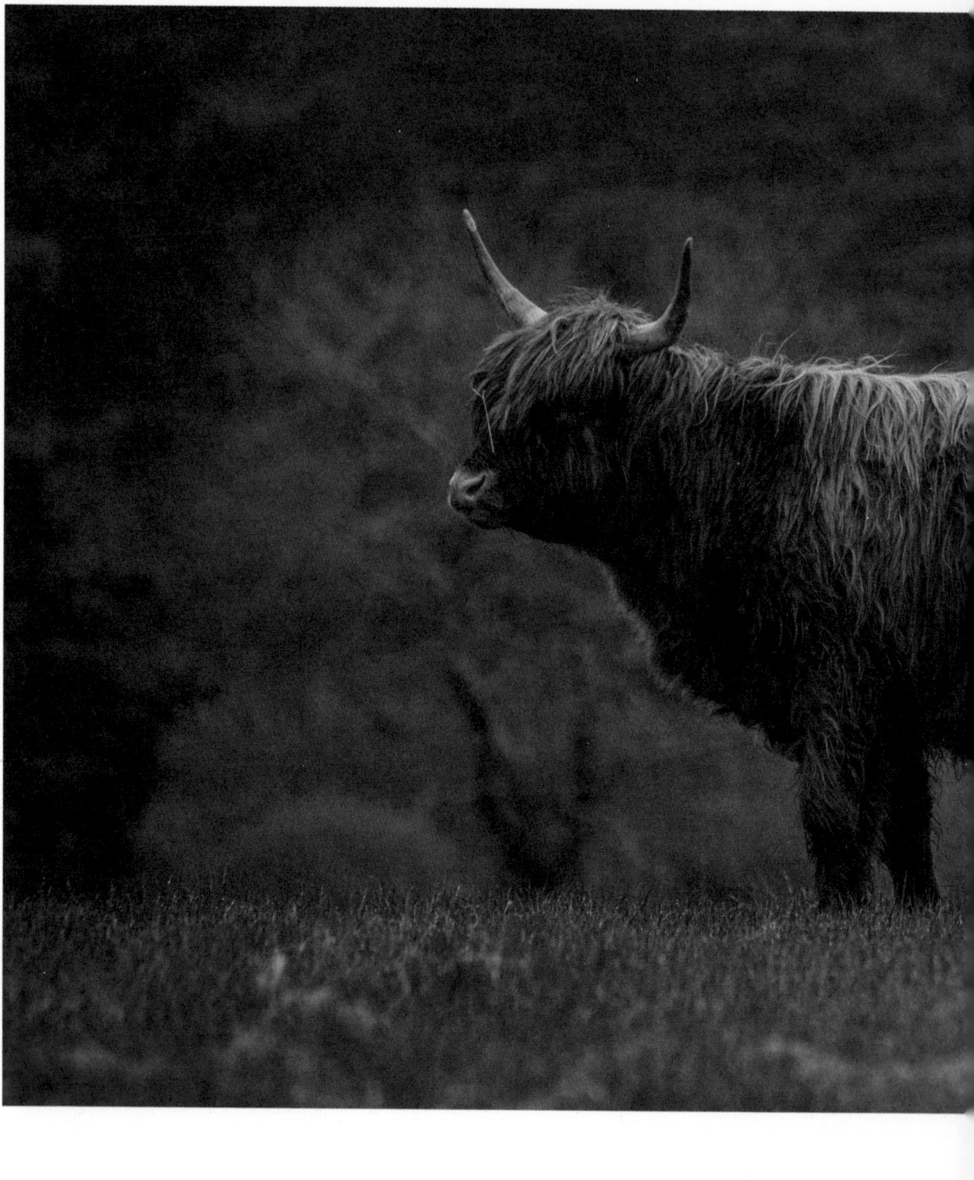

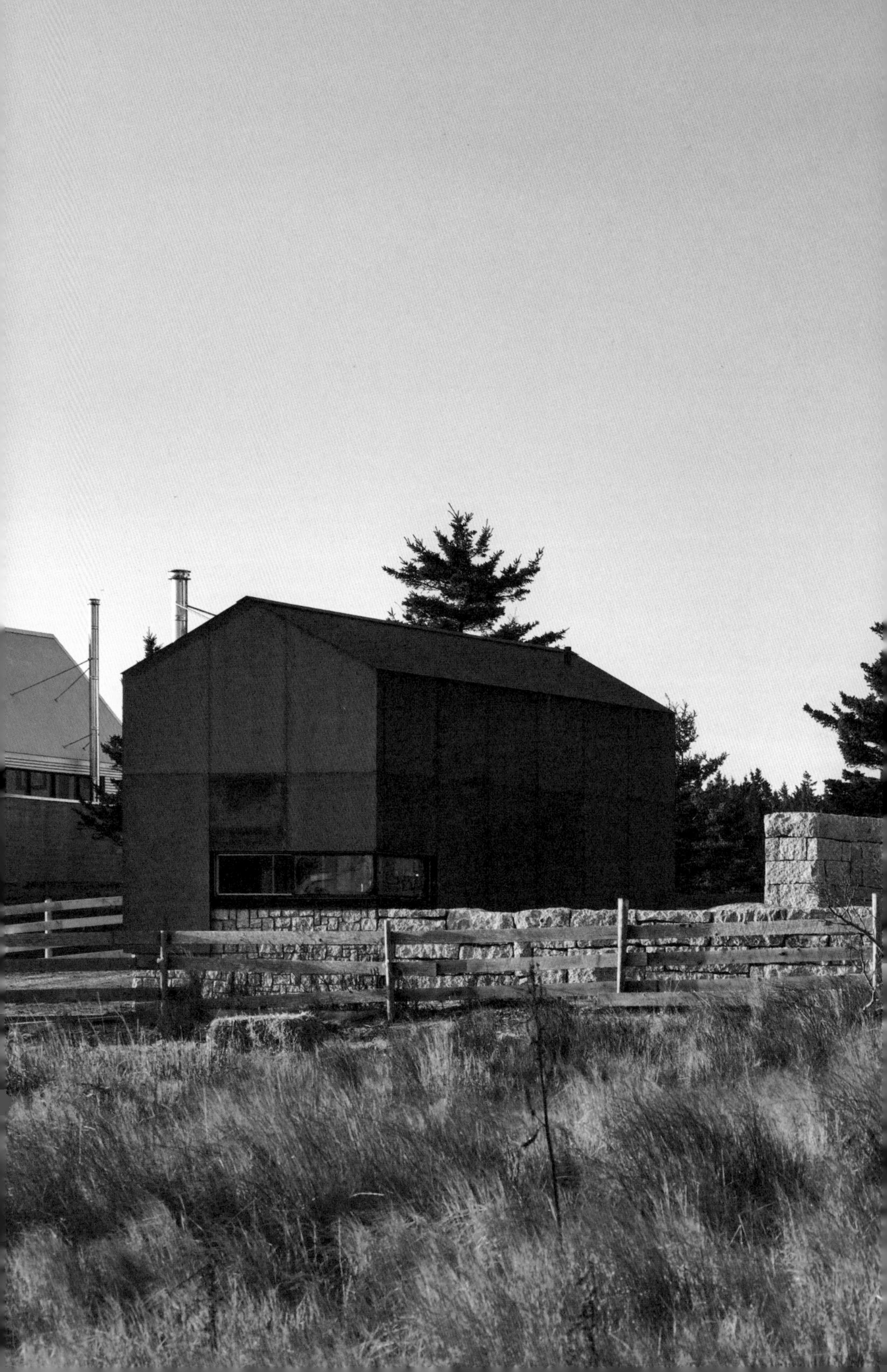

I-Q

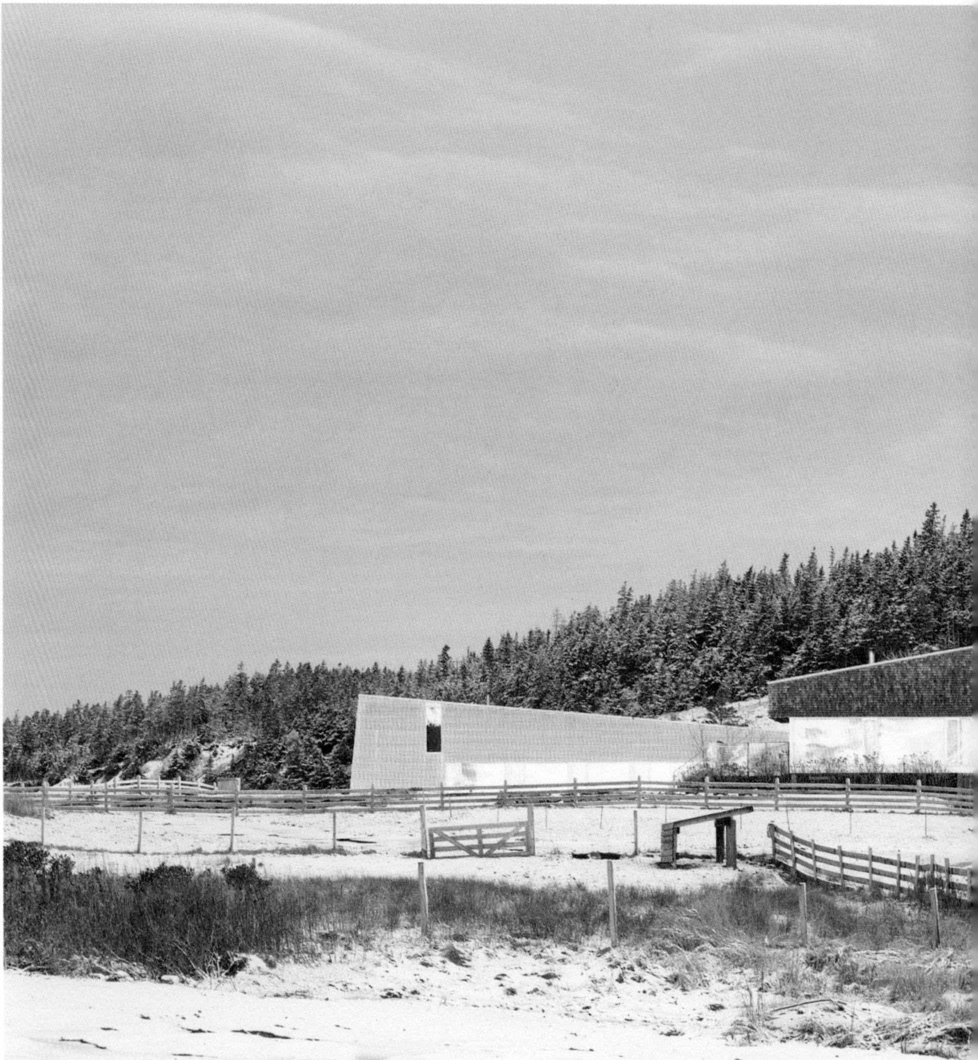

I-U

2
SkyRoom I

YOU'RE IN THE TREES. Alone in a skinny beam of sunlight that reaches you through the dense canopy.

The echo of tidal waters lapping at the shoreline.

Here predators of concern are known to come and go.

There's fresh scat from a large animal you need to kill and eat.

But you're not alone—

Behind you, loved ones: a partner you're bonded to, a crying child, a dying elder. And you're all part of a larger group, the clan of blood relations and others you've lived and traveled with for years.

You talk to the gods but they are of no practical use right now.

For too long your diet has been mostly berries and herbs. Your body is eating muscle.

March is the hungry month.

The days are still so short, so cold.

You're exhausted from being on the move—

On the border between life and death—

Will you make it to spring?

Imagine the first humans to settle in a permanent situation and finally stay put once and for all, *home sweet home*. What did they think about the spaces they created inside and between their buildings and on land they fenced and cultivated to grow food and raise animals? Comfort would have filtered into their priorities early on. Eventually too would higher-order priorities, a desire for a view of the mountains in the distance, a sublime expression of the shadows inside the temple, a balance between proximity and privacy in relation to neighbors.

More than anything else, the first village builders were motivated by a fear of consequence and a need for safety. And economy, too, making the most with the least, as shelter was a life-and-death matter.

Some lessons have been learned over millennia about how best to colonize our planet for human purposes. But it's not a radical soap-box revelation to say that we need to learn, and relearn, many more lessons in how we build and adapt communities at every scale. Despite the historical resiliency of our cities, our hubs of ingenuity and adaptiveness, their globalized economic dependencies—so dependent as they are on carbon and cyber fuels—are looking less sustainable and more brittle with each passing year and thus easier targets for bad actors of human, ecological, and epidemiological origin.

It's of consequence that, as sedentary as we've become, we're still on the move, just not our bodies, only our digital avatars. As if distance—and nature—no longer exists. As if our physical presence in built environments—other than the compulsion to complete ten thousand daily steps at the gym—isn't a material factor in our survival or the quality of our communities.

Maybe it's time that we all started thinking and acting again like those first village builders. We need their humble spirit of discovery—their pragmatism—before we discover it's too late.

Ever been a settler? Ever stood flat-footed on a frontier after a difficult journey into the unknown and built a community? A place to shelter your family and loved ones in a shining house on the hill? Or perhaps something less grandiose, a single room with a view and a shrine in the corner where you'd light sticks of incense to honor your good fortune and genuflect in the hopes of generating good karma?

Most of us are reasonably content to be occupants, owners, or renovators of what's already there.

Some build worlds out of nothing.

* * *

In the languid fogginess of an afternoon in late October, dusk nearly here, the air is breezeless and lonely for company. The leaves have turned psychedelic, the greens smeared in feverish swirls of red-orange. Smoke from village chimneys blends without a fight into the atmospheric grey. It's so eerily peaceful, until the silence is violated by a single bark from a dog in the woods, echoing longer than it should.

Then it's just me again, alone in the pastoral quiet, on my way to meet the architect Brian MacKay-Lyons. Our meeting spot is past the end of the public road in Upper Kingsburg near the farm that Brian and his wife Marilyn MacKay-Lyons bought decades ago, which now belongs to their daughter Ali and her husband Nathan. It's one of three small farms there that date from the 1750s, all hunkered down on the slope of a drumlin, a long hill perpendicular to the coastline, made of soil deposited by retreating Ice Age glaciers, a sensuous element in the undulating Nova Scotia landscape near the ocean.

The old farmhouse in question is a Cape Cod with barns and sheds out front and a long narrow field out back. It was one of Brian's first residential projects for which he inserted a dramatic lighthouse-lookout through the roof that hasn't survived the latest renovation done with his daughter. As he told me, wistfully, "The lookout had its day as a naive utopian gesture, and maybe was a mistake, ultimately. I still feel the ghost of it, what it meant for me as the essence of the ideal dwelling: providing a refuge with a prospect on the world."

Brian and I are getting together to talk about Shobac, a seaside village in a valley up the road from here, which he and Marilyn and their family have brought to life over many years now. The village has multiple identities. It's a showpiece for Brian's work as an architect, a sheep farm seasoned with a few cattle, and a high-end tourist retreat. Several of Brian's clients—seasonal visitors—own homes here that he designed. And for about twenty years, Shobac was home to Ghost Lab, a university summer school started by Brian for training architects through hands-on experience in building wood structures. Some of those structures are still standing, and integral to the look and purpose of Shobac today.

After the pavement ends, a gravel road takes me higher up the drumlin in a slow curve to the coast. In Ali's barnyard on my right, two horses are grooming one another as I walk past, and they pause to study me with equine aloofness. At the next bend, he comes into view, a solidly-built man in his mid-sixties with a purposeful gait. His wide face and intense blue eyes, and the head shaved bald, are disguised under sunglasses and a ball cap. He looks the part of a prosperous farmer who can both drive a tractor and conduct himself in a VIP lounge.

"Here's a question you won't like," I say, as we walk along, getting right into the ring with him, which we've done enough times in the twenty-five years we've been friends. "You've said innovation is overrated in architecture, that it's all fashion and novelty, 'the cult of the compelling object.' And that true originality requires a return to origins, to the forms that survive over time, and across cultures. So explain…"

I point to a building in a field behind us that, in the fog, appears broodingly distinct than the Cape Cod farm houses. It's a corrugated, metal box of industrial presence, virtually without external detail other than a ribbon window that splits the ocean-facing wall. The house tilts down the hill, hugging the land, making it seem like it's sliding down the slope. Designed for an old friend of Brian's, Sliding House is theatrical in its minimalist language and gleaming modernity applied to creating the illusion of downhill movement. It's a building I'm attracted to and yet repelled by. As the French say, *jolie laide*: alluring but not conventionally. A difficult beauty, but ugly to some folks around here.

"So, what origins are we talking about here, Brian?"

"I can lead the horse to water but can't make you drink," comes the quietly exasperated reply. "Look at my daughter's house just below it, the Cape Cod. It's a little crooked, having been pushed downhill for two hundred and fifty years by the prevailing westerly winds. But on the inside, we rebuilt it plumb as the day is long. Sliding House also tells the story of the wind and the slope of the land. Windswept outside, bullet-level plumb inside."

"It feels a little like a compelling object."

The provocation isn't fully working but he plays along. "It definitely tests the limits of being historic but in a modern and abstract way." 54

"I am not so sure about the history part."

"Could there be a more primary definition of history than the effects of nature on character? Look at the face of a fisherman after a life on the seas, or a Bedouin after years in the deserts. The wind made them and will eventually unmake them. Why can't a dwelling echo those forces, and speak to us by doing so?"

This gives him pause—to reload: "Look at any old barn or fishing shack around here. There's no waste or ornamental anything. This house, too. The tough, stripped-down exterior, the severity of it, makes it a piece of this place and culture. And yet, it also looks like a ship from outer space, from the future."

How Brian talks about the competing forces in his work has long intrigued me, his insistence that a building can be two—or more—viscerally different things at once. How can a home be both from the past and the future? From this planet and another?

Brian's most compelling buildings, which include Sliding House, have a relentless quality in balancing ideological directness with poetic economy. They could only exist as they are, certain of their identity.

They challenge you and invite questions about the story they have to tell. And in their answers, they don't take shit from anybody.

In conversations away from matters of architecture, Brian isn't as relentless or rhetorical. He has a gentler way of engaging you through a diplomatic folksiness and a well-tuned ear for listening that I associate with country-bred people who, while open enough, also know all things need not be revealed just because someone asks an invasive question or offers a reckless opinion. In his voice there's a subtle version of the Maritime dialect, with its sing-song cadence and ironic edges, stewed up from a linguistic chowder of Acadian, British and Indigenous influences that correspond to his lineage. There's a Métis background on his mother's side that allows him to credibly say his ancestors here go back thousands of years. "My Indigenous connection is distant but it's real. Look, we all choose who we want to be among the many things we are. In the Métis story of Atlantic Canada, there's a respect in that culture toward nature and the land—and a communal spirit—that I identify with and which informs everything I've ever built."

As we approach the coast, the fog starts to thin. While I can't see the ocean yet I feel the rhythmic thumping of waves collapsing into the dune beach. Up ahead, there's another of Brian's buildings, sited a safe distance back from the eroding clay cliffs two hundred feet above the beach. He designed the Campbell House as a younger architect, a modest gabled box under a silver metal roof, clad in grey shingles with white-trimmed windows, a respectful variation on the fishing shack that's so much a part of the scenery and folklore of Nova Scotia.

"Now there I see a more obvious connection to origins, Brian."

"It's a *good generic*, a good neighbor. A mentor of mine, a great architect, Glenn Murcutt, told me his buildings are semi-tailored garments. Eighty percent of the design comes from the material culture, and he only does the last twenty percent. In a place like Nova Scotia where there's amazing carpentry, thanks to hundreds of years building ships, you don't have to re-invent everything. Harnessing cultural genius is always more powerful than individual genius."

"It's a long way from Sliding House."

"And that's the point. It doesn't look like an architect's involved. Believe it or not, these small projects, as simple as they appear, provide insights that often end up in more visibly complex works...anyway, if you want to be the *village architect*, you have to serve many needs, solve different problems. You're like a country doctor. Some patients all they need is Vitamin C then off to bed. Others need brain surgery."

Buildings like the Campbell House, faithful to local building practices and design principles, work well in the Nova Scotia climate with its brutal wet-dry and freeze-thaw cycles. This house won't leak in torrential rains that go horizontal in a Category 2 storm. It won't crack in the spring after the ice melts. It will hold the heat in winter and cool you in summer. It's an essay in economic logic in about four hundred square feet, sleeps six, and has the structural fortitude of a tiny lobster boat, capable of staying afloat in rough seas. It feels like a place where you'd retreat after a life-changing event, where hours would be spent fussing with the wood stove, thinking about things with a little more humility or resolve to do better.

I ask him how something so simple can say so much to me.

"It's telling you where you've come from, Larry. Our ancestors by and large came to North America with nothing. Survival was everything. Sustainability meant doing things you could not afford to get wrong. A good generic was vital, being able to build a place without making it up as you went along. Your life depended on it."

* * *

Within a gauntlet of trees, there's an opening before us, the road dipping down through heavy green, and so down we go with it, lower and then lower still, bridging a wetland and the gurgling stream within it. Soon we're climbing again up another steep drumlin, my gaze forced up towards the emptiness of blue sky until a solitary crow ink-blots the view, cawing indignantly at who knows what.

Up on the drumlin ridge, there's another of Brian's client homes, Messenger House II. It's a long, narrow building with a monopitched roof that rises up to confront the Atlantic beyond, slashing through airspace. A blade of a building, wedge-shaped, not a bit of fat on it. Imagine a lighthouse on its side. It's more accessible to my sensibility than the gliding rectangularity of Sliding House. It reads as a launching pad for the gaze to rise along its length, up towards sky and eventually to where sky meets horizon. It has a muscular presence, but not like a concrete bunker or stone castle. More like a kite, the wing of a large bird, thin-skinned, but wiry-strong under the shingled bravado. "It looks vulnerable up there, a wood skeleton, just sticks, really, with a few steel veins," Brian says. "But it has amazing tensile strength."

Brian built this house using a strategy that he'll repeat several times at Shobac: selling buildable property lots to people who he and Marilyn believe will make good neighbors, but only if they agree to have their homes designed by Brian and their land used as grazing pasture. It's the architect as developer, village builder, farmer, de facto mayor and, at times, social director.

We gain the ridge as dusk intensifies, bathing everything in soft rosy light. In the field to our left, four Highland cattle—sensitive animals of shaggy gold massiveness—silently monitor us.

And there it is, directly below us: Shobac.

The village has risen up in a seaside valley of some fifty acres, including hillside pastures, hemmed in from behind by the drumlin we're standing on now and from the front by the LaHave River estuary as it bleeds into the open Atlantic. On our far left, below the drumlin, and beyond a tidal pond, there's a rock dune beach. It leads to the forested Gaff Point headland that, from this vantage point, looks like some gigantic manta ray, brooding on a waveless sea.

On our right, on much higher land, there's a border of trees, the entrance to the woods that lead to Lower LaHave several kilometres upriver. Back there it's all towering cliffs on land that, so long ago, was granted by the British Crown to one Christian Shoubach, who provided the MacKay-Lyons family with the inspiration to name their land, their farm, Shobac.

As I look down at the twenty (at last count) buildings in the architectural inventory of the valley, I feel like an intrepid explorer discovering a civilization the world knows nothing about. It's like something unique and hidden is being revealed. A secret colony, perhaps, where something esoteric is being studied or accomplished, all requiring formal separation from the rest of us.

Something inside me always expands when I pause here to contemplate the shift in elevation from drumlin height to valley depth while I scan the horizon and the ocean vastness beyond.

From this distance, high on the drumlin, Shobac appears to be monumental Land Art, each structure part of a larger sculptural ensemble, which is true, given that everything comes from the vision of one architect. Here you encounter buildings that, like Sliding House and Messenger House II, test design limits along with quieter works like the Campbell House that openly speak to history. Providing gravitas to the scene are two orphaned buildings that were rescued from destruction and brought here to be rehabilitated: the octagonal 1880s Troop Barn from the Annapolis Valley, and the 1830s Schoolhouse, the classic one-room deal with a double-pitched gable roof that came from a village near the one where Brian grew up, close to Nova Scotia's southern tip, which Brian reminds me is a landscape very similar to Shobac.

"As a young man, you think you're leaving home for good, on a journey to the ends of the Earth to follow your ambition, but it's funny how sometimes you end up where you started," he says. "That's the power of landscape and those community influences that shape you."

As we saunter down into the valley, the experience awakens in me an emotion akin to the undergraduate wonder I recall from sitting in darkened seminar rooms so many years ago, as one slide after another introduced me to the archeological treasures—the citadels, palaces, and lost cities—of the ancient world. In Greece, at Mycenae, Knossos and the Acropolis in Athens. The mudbrick cities of the Near East. Persepolis in Shiraz. The Anasazi cliff palaces in Arizona.

For me, Shobac has the time-defying resonance of those historic ruins in the archeological canon. For something so contemporary in architectural terms, Shobac conveys the idea that what exists here today is connected to the deep past.

* * *

Like so much of the Americas, Shobac sits on land that was inhabited thousands of years before any Europeans arrived.

The history of Indigenous habitation here, and excavations of their artifacts, whatever they might be, haven't yet been a sustained focus of research or archeological work at or near Shobac. I haven't heard of any shell heap excavations or discoveries here of tools and weapons consistent with Indigenous settlement. The written accounts of life in the Shobac area—who the settlers were, how they lived, what they believed—only start coming down to us from the later 1700s.

This land, this valley, in its more recent history since Europeans settled down here in a permanent way, has been called different names, depending on who lived here and when: Mosher's Settlement, the Shore, the Back Shore, and now Shobac.

What we do have as clues to life in the deeper past here are about a dozen granite foundations, some arguably going back to the 1500s and the first European settlements among the Mi'kmaq, as illustrated on the first maps of the so-called New World by Samuel de Champlain when he made landfall here in 1604. One map shows a number of European houses, complete with smoking chimneys, among a network of teepees in or near the valley. Were these homes built by the earliest French traders who were known to intermarry with the Mi'kmaq? Portuguese fishermen? Basque whalers? British privateers?

In the early 2000s the foundations were evaluated more methodically, Brian tells me, by archeologists who came to Shobac to study migration patterns from Europe. They concluded there were stone foundations here since at least the 1500s. Brian claims that one of his long-deceased friends here, the village elder and farmer Albert Oxner, often talked about the "French foundations from the French time."

59

But other than Brian there hasn't been much enthusiasm among the few chroniclers of local history for the idea that the foundations today go back to Champlain, or earlier to older European settlements. A view often expressed in the limited written material available on Shobac is that the foundations are artifacts of the first Swiss-German settlers from the 1750s. *No French history here, folks, nothing to see, now move along.* It's true that the granite in the ground reflects a site scheme consistent with Swiss-German settlement here. It's also true in agrarian cultures worldwide that stones from older habitations were recycled into newer ones. Granite block, sized for a foundation, was an extremely valuable resource.

Who has the better claim on history? I'm not sure how to answer that. Everyone who ever lived here is the only truly ethical answer. Another answer—harsh in its sweeping disregard for the untold stories of one culture or another—is that history belongs to those who write it, or at least remember it and pass their stories on....

The locally contested part of Shobac history, however, relates mainly to the provenance of the granite foundations. How old are they? Who built the houses? Do they go back to Champlain's time or earlier?

It's plausible that the region was a trading hub well before the 1750s. In the 1600s the area was hopping with intrigue, commerce, and conflicts both open and covert. And the French explorers were in the thick of it. In 1631, the capital of New France in North America was briefly located near Shobac, right across the LaHave River estuary, moved there from Port-Royal by the governor at the time, Issac de Razilly, to exploit seaborne trade opportunities.

My thinking is: you know there are ghosts in the air and under your feet here. It ultimately doesn't matter to me who they are.

* * *

When Brian and I reach the valley floor, the road hives off in all directions, leaving us in a small village square.

Right in front of us, there's a gabled gem of a cottage, sheathed in rust-red Corten. One critic said it had the charm and immediacy of a child's crayon drawing. In fact, Brian was inspired by one such drawing that his daughter Ali produced as a youngster. The house features generous main-floor windows that take a large bite out of one corner of the building, providing views of the pastures around it. For something so small, its impact is big, given its pivotal position in the valley. It was named Enough House, an outcome of research in Brian's practice to design an affordable housing prototype that could be easily customized. It's an attempt to answer the question, what's *enough house* in these sustainability-obsessed times? It's now called the Gatehouse, the Shobac welcoming committee in built form. You half-expect someone to emerge from it to lead a guided tour. For all its steel-clad modernity, the Gatehouse is basically a good generic.

To the left of the Gatehouse, across a gap of twenty paces, the Schoolhouse provides another anchoring element of the village square. Brian and Marilyn often live there—or camp out, which is more like it—when it isn't being rented to guests. It's a box under a gable, and right out of central casting as the one-room schoolhouse, although the interior has been renovated into a well-appointed cottage. "As a child, I admired this classical structure just down the road from where I grew up," Brian says. "It seemed like the missing link between domestic and public architecture. Domestic in scale and materials, but public in program and pretension. Both modest and monumental."

Turning further to our left, there's the Troop Barn with its forty-

60

foot ceiling height, a dignified post-and-beam octagon with a majesti-
cally cavernous interior where you wouldn't think twice about holding
a wedding, a seminar, a concert, or a road hockey game. It's done all
that and more. The first time I was inside it, years back, Brian turned
to me, then scanned the room, inviting me to do the same, as if I were
in danger of missing the point. "When I stand here, it's like I'm in a
poor man's Pantheon," he said. "You ever wonder how much different
a barn-raising is from building a cathedral?"

"I guess, uh, scale, materials, the Pope's blessing?"

"Think about it. *Basilica* is just a Roman word for barn."

* * *

MacKay-Lyons is a Canadian word for architect.

Today Brian is renowned internationally for a body of work built
over forty-plus years, mainly in Nova Scotia, where he's been a life-
long resident except for stints, much earlier in his career, working
in important practices and studying on multiple continents. Distinguished critics have written books about him on blue-chip imprints.
For decades he's held visiting professorships at leading universities
while holding tenure at Dalhousie as a full professor. He's produced
several books of his own. His firm has won over a hundred awards of
significance. The recognition Brian gets these days increasingly comes
with the sobriquet of *lifetime achievement*. In 2015, he was awarded the
Gold Medal from the Royal Architectural Institute of Canada, the
highest honor in Canada for an architect.

Raised in a small Nova Scotia village along the Chebogue River,
Arcadia, his life was bigger from the get-go. His father, a local mer-
chant, was a World War Two veteran, a Knights of Columbus and
scoutmaster type, a community bigwig, his mother a homemaker, the
softer and more soulful parent. There was an appetite for culture in
the family, jazz, antiques, history, travel. On a childhood trip to Rome,
four-year old Brian and his older brother David together wrapped their
arms around an ancient column. As Brian tells it, he knew then he was
destined to become an architect. He jokes that he arrived at that insight
late compared to Frank Lloyd Wright whose mother knew her son
would be an architect, as the story goes, when he was still in her womb.

As a child, Brian fought a learning disability that made it difficult to absorb the written word and forced him to become, he says, an oral learner and good listener. His erudition beyond architecture—anthropology, history, philosophy, art, science—speaks to a lifetime of learning. With difficulty reading, how did he do it? "By asking questions before opening my mouth," he says forcefully. "And by listening to my elders, respecting people who know things. A lost art."

His architectural practice, now in its fourth decade, produces work that embodies the globalized values of contemporary Modernism fused to the historically local. Certainly earlier in his career, his buildings featured a distinctly regional vocabulary that emphasized local building practices and materials as an argument against—and ideological resistance to—the forces of globalization and mobile capital that, he felt, weren't always benign in creating good buildings and communities.

In the voluminous critical recognition of his work, Brian has laid down a quotable mythology of his philosophy as an architect. But don't expect a Michael Ondaatje novel of his personal journey, the recollections of unruly teenaged behavior, the insights into the hills and valleys of psychological growth, the tormented confessions of doubt when failure demanded a moment in his story. That's not how he rolls.

"There should be some separation between public and private life, otherwise you have neither, you have a narcissistic cultural disaster," he says. "I know it's a common impulse these days but I'm not one for displaying my gonads out there on the front lawn."

For the momentary sake of argument, let's say there's a material difference between one's external persona and inner character. Between the two, in Brian's case, there's a well-calibrated mediating function, what might be called discretion in what he's willing to reveal about himself. A gifted storyteller also gifted at controlling his story.

I've wondered at times what he's like with no one else around.

I got my voyeuristic moment at the end of a cold winter day at Shobac. We had spent the afternoon, warmed by a hardwood fire in the wood stove of the Studio, talking about Leon Battista Alberti, the prototypical Renaissance man, philosopher, architect, artist, cryptographer, and mathematician. Alberti argued that architecture and the design of the city in particular was the most notable art form of a civilization, an inspiration in Brian's thinking about urbanism.

Later, approaching dusk, in the biting wind and subzero cold, as I was walking home over the hills, maybe ten minutes after leaving the Studio, I heard Brian's tractor rumbling. When I turned back towards the sound, I saw the man-machine emerge on a drumlin ridge, a shrink-wrapped hay bale impaled on the forklift. The cattle were waiting for him. Dinner time. Against the setting sun, he materialized as a stick figure in silhouette. On the wind came the sonic residue of a man talking to his animals. Fragments of words I couldn't make out.

One minute we're in Renaissance Italy together, discussing the history of architecture, the next he's alone on the North Atlantic coast, a farmer in overalls, hard at work on a frozen evening at a time in the narrative of our civilization that has reduced the family farm to an anachronism in our agribusiness-driven planet. As brief as that moment was, it came to me with some force that, at Shobac, while the architecture will always be the showstopper, the farm is equally a meaningful expression of Brian's dreams for this place.

Doggedly, at Shobac, Brian has summoned an agrarian world lost, as they say, in the ruins of time. This place wasn't much when Brian and Marilyn acquired the land but a drain on money and time. It was an abandoned village nobody wanted, virtually worthless, nothing but old foundations, overgrown fields, remembered by few, celebrated by fewer. In Brian's obsession to build a life here, he understood the relevance and power of the past—buried under his feet and within himself—that have made him, as a farmer, a man looking at the future.

* * *

In these pages I'm not attempting a forensic account of Brian's career that positions him critically in his profession. That work has been underway for many years now. My interest is what he's achieved at Shobac with Marilyn and their family as an enterprise that has unfolded over more than three decades, an accomplishment of what's possible in constructing a community on your own terms.

But what kind of community is it?

Shobac today isn't, realistically assessed, a village of many full-time residents or with civic status as such. Nor does it have a diverse economy operating with scale. Neither is it a resort of the full-service variety. It has historic foundations in the ground but it's not an archeological dig. It's a working farm, but a small one, mainly sheep. The main attraction is the architecture. The tourists who stay here do so, in large part, because they have a taste for what's been built and the landscape around it.

What I do claim, however, is that Shobac belongs in the first rank of intentional or experimental communities built by architects of historic importance. As an expression of Brian's gifts as an architect, Shobac draws comparisons to Frank Lloyd Wright's Taliesen compounds in Wisconsin and Arizona, Donald Judd's art sanctuary in Marfa, Texas and the Sea Ranch community in Northern California.

In that celebrated context, Shobac, as it exists today and as a work in perpetual progress, is a community of ideas—a living manifesto—in how landscape, climate, culture and architecture can work together in elevating our experience in the built environment.

* * *

In the waning evening light, there's still so much to see.

Near the Troop Barn, there are views of a spit about half a football-field length that projects into the tidal lake behind the rock dunes. Brian calls the area the fishing port. It features a cluster of new homes—some clad in wood, others in metal—built for Brian's clients. There's a boathouse, too, that belongs to the MacKay-Lyons family. The homes are built close together, with exterior spaces that make the most of the sun and the least of the wind. It's a village in its own right, inspired by the fishing port that was there until the early 70s.

Of course it's not a fishing village in any sense that a fisherman could practically relate to. The houses convey visual echoes of the fishing shack form, but these are sleek instruments of elite architectural design, every view and detail labored over. And if there's work going on in these buildings, it has nothing to do with fishing. This isn't about proximity to the sea as a source of physical survival but for visual meditation or voyeuristic recreation. In a traditional Maritime fishing village, a house might have one water-facing window where, as the story goes, wives and mothers would fretfully turn their gaze throughout the day, hoping to see their men returning from the dangerous workplace of the sea. Many of the sea-facing windows in this fishing port are wall-sized glass curtain. You're not likely to find a disassembled boat or truck engine in the yards here, but rather a hot tub or pizza oven.

At the opposite end of the valley from the fishing port, dramatically prominent there near the cliffs is the Studio, a first cousin to Messenger House II, a corrugated metal wedge with a monopitched roof that rises up toward the estuary. In addition to being a dining hall, the Studio is a satellite office for Brian's practice. It forms a courtyard in the heart of the valley with a terrace of four rental cabins beside it. There's a Barn behind the Studio birthed from the sensibility that produced Sliding House, a long box that features a corrugated metal sleeve wrapping a wood structure built on poles. It appears to rotate toward you, an abstracted wave, frozen at the peak before crashing. A landscape wave, with bigger waves being the terraced hills, curdling up behind it.

* * *

In the darkness, Brian has left me to wander on my own.

At the village square, I saunter through the gap between the Schoolhouse and the Gatehouse towards the cliffs. I enter the courtyard where, on my right, there are four rental cabins in tight formation. Each looks like two buildings in one: a box half-inserted into a larger shed with a roof that slides down toward the water.

In the far corner of the courtyard near the Studio, there's an old foundation, possibly there before the time of Champlain's map. Right now it's all floodlit from within, breathing yellow light up into the darkness, drawing me towards it. Through a slot in the granite blocks that form a one-foot border above the foundation, I head down a granite staircase to the all-granite brick floor. These aren't the interlocking bricks you get at the garden centre. They're all hand cut, textured, a salt-and-pepper grey, and the effect is that of a floor that feels weighty, a surface with a long history and the scars to prove it.

Years ago when I saw this foundation for the first time, it was not just a ruin but ruined, the walls collapsing, stones tumbled one on top the other, grasses growing out of crevices, a few hunks of charred wood left over from a bonfire. And now, with the work done by masons brought in for another project here, Brian and Marilyn have rebuilt the foundation with a mixture of old stones and new granite, completely changing the feel of the place. Rechristened SkyRoom, the foundation now suggests the word *chamber*, a place for rituals, its demeanor more formal or ceremonial for what is basically a hole in the ground.

Down here I'm startled to hear the ocean with much more clarity, which I guess is what happens when you take away a sense like sight. You enhance another sense.

It really is a starry, starry night.

Being here in the SkyRoom, looking up, which is what you're supposed to do, puts me in mind of the Light and Space artist James Turrell and the rooms he constructs for viewing, ideally in meditative silence, the changing voices of the sky in the American Southwest.

I have this desire to fall onto my back and look up into the panorama of distant light sheltered in more distant darkness.

This space takes me back, in spirit, to the *dromos*, a roofless passage cut into a hill at the Bronze Age citadel at Mycenae that leads to a massive beehive tomb inside. When I walked that passageway so long ago now, lined on both sides with ashlar stone, I experienced a version of *phantom limb* as if the excavated dirt were still there, enveloping me in the ghosts from the past. It's a feeling I've had at the Vietnam War Memorial in Washington, where two long black granite walls, joined into a loose V-shape, inscribed with the names of American soldiers who died in that war, were inserted into a modest slope and the land taken away from the interior of the V. When you walk that interior you feel surrounded by absence and loss. Here, too, I feel enclosed by weighty invisible forces.

66

In the quiet of the coastal night, my sense of being in the present is dissolving. This foundation has endured centuries of cycles of growth and decay. Reborn again as SkyRoom, it's alive as more than a foundation that once held up structure, as more than a ruin left to its own devices. As reconstructed, as a place within the landscape for congregation and conversation, where there's little else to see but the people with you and the sky above, the SkyRoom offers an invitation to look inward. As I submit to that impulse, I do so thinking that this ruin deserves a more elaborate myth of its journey here.

3
Mythic House

I

H

A

G

G

G

G

E

E

$\overline{}$ *toise*

100 200 300 400

Les chifres montrent les braſſes d'eau.

ux	D Vne baſſe a l'entree du port	H Vne riuiere qui va dans le
E Vne petite iſle couuerte de	terres 6, ou 7. lieux. auec
bois.	peu d'eau.
e-	F Le Cap de la Héue.	I Vn eſtang proche de la
es	G Vne baye ou il y a quanti-	mer.
té d'iſles couuertes de bois.

April 1594

IN THE BLACKEST HOUR, she finds herself awake, seeing nothing but feeling trapped inside the four walls. The man next to her struggles in his sleep, mumbling in the language he came to her with. So there she lies, the Great Spirit flooding into her. She imagines her body as a river fed from undiscoverable sources. All she can recall now of the dream is a white feather that flowers up from a helmet of gleaming silver. Why it terrifies her she doesn't yet know. The task right now is to serve the Great Spirit by etching the vision into stone.

She breathes in the scent of the fire dying in the hearth, tasting ash floating in the dampness. The dog at her feet flattens his ears towards her, sensing she's about to get up. Once on her feet, her eyes seeing through darkness, she moves silently through the room. At the back door she reaches for a shawl, then slips outside, into the vegetable garden, the dog at her heels, the dew tickling her bare feet as she walks along the stone path to the gate, escaping into thick fog that glows in light from the full moon.

The windless night is alive with the echo of low tide gurgling over the stones terraced on the shore.

She glances back at the house, snug in a clearing among the trees. It's a place where she rarely sleeps the night through, often waking like she does tonight, struggling to breathe.

He built the house after she took him as a husband. A one-room gabled box over a cellar of granite block, surrounded by the wigwams of her people in this valley beside the sea. South-facing, the house is warmed by the sun most days. In the garden, there is respite from the prevailing winds. The fence he built has created spaces that didn't exist before, where she spends her days harvesting, washing clothes, kept company by the dog. In the yard, she feels that time passes differently, slower at times, faster at others. There are times the experience is blissful. There are times she feels lost, cut off. She's still not comfortable with his idea of living here all year, a source of tension between them.

That's never how they've lived, moving as the seasons change. As much as she respects what he's built for them, she struggles with another idea of his: that the house, as a permanent dwelling with fenced-in territory, is *theirs*, not something shared. She insisted that anyone in the community can use the house to do business with the traders.

In the dense fog, she gazes up towards the invisible moon, then starts walking up the steep trail through the trees, soon reaching a small clearing on the drumlin ridge. Up here the night sky is star-filled and clear. The fog below shape-shifts, breaking open here, closing there, swirling with unknowable purpose, just like the Great Spirit, she thinks, flowing around her, providing glimpses into hidden worlds and meanings without revealing everything at once. She climbs the small platform that he built for her to work on, another private place, offering views to the horizon, which to everyone else seemed a waste of time and wood, although she's observed that some now regularly come up here just to sit, gossip, and take in those wasteful views. The platform is a raft of pine on posts.

In a circle around her are a dozen small slabs of thin grey slate, etched with her latest drawings.

72

Three years ago he'd stayed behind when the ship went back across the endless water, presenting himself to her with a hammer, a chisel, a leather bag with a half-dozen handmade nails, a copper pot under his arm. When they undressed the first time under the cliffs at the secret beach, she discovered the scar on his hip where the musket had struck him years back. She was drawn to the peaceful quality of his eyes, his willingness to leave everything behind to be with her, including his God.

Their liaison caused strife in the clan. She had suitors upset by her favoring a white man. He was threatened more than once and for a while the women shunned her. They prevailed because of her mother's influence, a healer renowned across the Mi'kmaq world. He proved adept at winning over her kin, learning their language and customs, always showing respect for the elders while teaching people how the Europeans think, helping them trade more profitably. He increased his prestige by building the ramp from the shore to help the traders—New Englanders, Basque, French, Portuguese—more easily bring their cod catches up for drying and salting atop the long stretches of fish flakes, the *vigneaux*, along the cape.

Down by the pond, she hears the younger men, her brothers among them, the men with no wives yet, all telling lies about whose arrows killed the moose they tracked last winter. They're steaming mussels around a fire before heading out fishing. For generations her people have spent the summers here trading with the Europeans, before migrating upriver each fall in their birch canoes to endure the winter in the forest. In the smoke that reaches her from the fire she guesses the mix of wood that feeds it. A game she plays with her husband that he never wins. So there she sits, alone, eyes closed, imagining the elements of the fire while the wordless residue of the Great Spirit's story settles into her. As if in trance she meditates through the night until sunrise. Below her, in the valley, the fog hasn't yielded sovereignty over what can be seen there.

And now, feeling purified, she begins etching into stone the image of a feather flowering out of a helmet. She can't visualize the man who wears the helmet but knows he's a warrior.

Time doesn't pass until the dog barks, announcing that her husband will emerge from the trees, and so he does with a cup of birch tea to help with her morning sickness. The fog has risen with him, clouding her views of the ocean and the sun. He sits at her feet, leaning back into her, and together they stare into the dramatic nothingness. She gazes into the blackness of his hair, slick with condensing fog, running her fingers through it. They are content in the blindness of the moment.

The dog, bored by their enjoined stillness, scampers off through the trees towards the pond and the indulgence of her brother who will feed him a hunk of smoked mackerel.

A gust shudders through the trees, causing fog to dissipate, opening up horizon views across the ocean now in sunlight. As they take everything in, connected by touch and silence to one another, to an alliance deepened by the child within her, there's a shared sense of gratitude for this moment stolen from the coming day. It will be calm on the shore, so he'll gather up sea manure that washed in with the last storm and shovel the stuff into their gardens, sweetening the earth. She'll pick berries with the women and tell them today or possibly tomorrow about the child, although of course they suspect it. When she does, they'll say she needs to move out of the house into the moon wigwam, fearing that otherwise she will drain the energies of her husband as she purifies herself to bring life into the world.

73

Today at dusk she will plant the etching in the ground along the garden path, and not give it a second thought for years.

May 1604

From up on the ridge, on her etching platform, they catch a glimpse of the tall ship, white-sailed, angling into the estuary after slicing past the headland where the Portuguese camped last year.

Turning to her, he says, "It does not matter who comes and what gifts they bring. I am forever of this place and of you."

She smiles at his pledge, how forcefully he still wants her to believe that he's left the old world behind, forever, for his life here with her and her family, their two daughters and son.

Their marriage has survived her taking the children and moving out of the house into her own wigwam after her mother's death. Initially he couldn't accept she'd given up on making the house their home. She claimed the nightmares came too often, and anyway living there had worsened the rift with her siblings. Alone he brooded for months in the house. He was in danger again of being attacked by other men after the night the traders staying with him got drunk and unruly and made lewd advances to the young women who brought them food. He saved his reputation and his life, barely, by stealing a musket from the visitors and marching them to their boat. Soon after he begged to move into her wigwam, deciding once and for all to gift the house to the community for the exclusive purpose of doing business with outsiders. If it could not be her home, it could not be his.

"They will keep coming," she says, glancing past him at the ship now visible at the mouth of the bay. "They will, my love."

* * *

The expedition leader, the French nobleman Pierre Dugua, *sieurs de Mons*, vigorous at fifty, paces the quarterdeck while watching the two skiffs from his ship rowing away on a placid morning sea, a half dozen men on each. In an affably sardonic voice, he shouts, "Champlain, when visiting the camp, it would be advisable to go in armor. Regardless, do

74

not go ashore without the Swiss *arquebusiers* at your side. Your scalp belongs where it is now, on your head."

"Sieur de Mons, your concern is respectfully noted," comes the equally sardonic reply from Champlain in the lead skiff.

Sitting ramrod straight in the stern, wearing common soldier's garb, Champlain is a solidly muscular presence in his later thirties, high forehead, receding hairline, prominent nose, intense eyes, a face ornamented in scars sufficient enough to justify his reputation as a man of action, a leader of men in battle. "We go forward in the spirit of peace and harmony," he announces, less sardonic now, but not looking back once to his mentor on the ship, gesturing for one of the men to drop the lead line for a depth reading. Then he holds up his astrolabe to calculate the position of the sun.

Dugua shakes his head, pleasantly confounded as he has been before by Champlain's unflappability, his relentless optimism in the teeth of the unknown and, at times, the unmistakably threatening. "Champlain, as a Son of the King of France, may the Lord's divine favor bless you on your endeavors today," he says raising a flask of cognac to his lips for a drink from the best of his family's cellar.

"Sieurs de Mons, be assured the spirit of exploration shall not be compromised by a lack of caution. Peace begets peace."

This is a welcome statement to the men, uncertain what to make of the word play between their commander and the King's cartographer. They're tense with the possibility of confronting the Mi'kmaq on their first day at anchor after the three-week crossing. Especially on edge are the Swiss mercenaries, some still at the mercy of lingering seasickness, all bunched into one skiff, each with a wheel-lock *arquebus*, a self-igniting rifle of consequence. For now, they have put their trust in Champlain who commands respect by being quietly confident and disciplined, rarely superior in demeanor, even though he's a nobleman in the good graces of the King, and rumored to be his illegitimate son.

As the day unfolds, Champlain orchestrates the mapping exercise with skills honed from years navigating dangerous coastlines on sea voyages with his father and uncle. On this mission, as the King's cartographer, he's also working with Dugua to find a proper site for a permanent colony of French settlers in what they will come to call

75

New France. Dugua also has other considerations to distract him: developing his ten-year monopoly on the fur trade from the King.

In the fog they drift towards shore and the sound of surf lazily sloshing over shoal rock. When the fog suddenly clears, the Mi'kmaq camp comes boldly into view: a clearing on a valley floor featuring wigwams set back from the cliffs, fronting the slope of a wooded drumlin. Champlain expected something like this, but not the house. The work of Europeans. He reaches for his telescope and, to his surprise, there's a man in European peasant clothing among the Mi'kmaq anticipating their arrival, some with weapons at the ready, bow and arrow, spears, axes.

"Let us go ashore," he orders.

As they glide in on the gentle tide, he turns to the second skiff holding the armed Swiss soldiers, and shouts, "Gentlemen, stay where you are, for now, as it will only cause trouble to present ourselves with weapons. Stay there until requested."

The men are unhappy that he appears to be going against the counsel of Dugua. Going to the Mi'kmaq camp, he knows, is a necessary act of diplomacy while in the area. But it must be done right, regardless of the risks, which Champlain thinks are minimal. These Mi'kmaq have been trading for generations with Europeans of many nations, peacefully. Dugua trusts him to do what's right.

As the boat wedges into the sandy bottom of the shallows at the edge of the spit, Champlain leaps over the gunwales and strolls ashore, ahead of his men, giving the impression of not having a care in the world. On dry land, kicking wet sand from his boots, he pauses in his advance, wondering who will come forward to greet him. Meanwhile, the men in Champlain's skiff, having pulled the boat ashore, climb out and fall in behind their leader, all tentative.

It's the European who separates from about two dozen Mi'kmaq men and women. Champlain, weaponless, walks up to the man and a handshake soon connects them.

"Jean Poirier," the man says in French.

"Samuel Champlain, sir, of Brouage. And you."

"I was born in Toulouse. But as a young man I moved south, to the mountains," he says in a dialect Champlain identifies with the Basque. "In the Kingdom of Navarre."

"So you are French and more, perhaps," Champlain replies.

In his mid-thirties now, Poirier, like Champlain, is a compact figure rippling with energy and possessed of an engaging smile. After Champlain reclaims his hand, he stands at ease with himself and the situation, wondering if he'll be invited to visit the camp.

"Poirier, on which vessel did you make your way here?"

"A whaler, sir, sailing from San Sebastian."

"The whaling trade has not been thriving recently."

"For thirteen years now I've been here, my home."

"So now, you are a citizen of this new world, Poirier. And we are here to introduce ourselves. Let us begin there."

Poirier, looks back to the crowd behind him, and sees that his wife is approaching, a regal presence draped in beautifully stitched animal skins, embroidered in a motif of swirling eagles.

"My wife, Muin'iskw," Poirier says. "Our chief."

"Welcome to our home, after your long voyage," Muin'iskw says in a neutral voice.

"Madam, you speak beautiful French," Champlain says in a rough Mi'kmaq dialect picked up on last year's voyage.

For Muin'iskw, it's the first time a European has addressed her in a language close to her own. She decides to be impressed. Her husband notices the change in her, the internalized reaction, and, catching her eye, lets her know it with a wink, a habit she has yet to break him of.

"You speak of this new world as you call it," she says as she turns to walk up through the dunes and past the lines of fish flakes, expecting everyone to follow, which they do. "Our people have been living here with our gods for time beyond your counting. It is a very old world from where we greet visitors from your newer world."

Champlain, reverting to French, says, "Madam, I mean no grievous insult to your profound history here."

"For many thousands of years they have lived here," Poirier pipes in with enthusiasm. "To a time before—"

"Before Christ," Champlain says.

"Well before, sir."

Muin'iskw often toys with European visitors by speaking their languages as a way of mocking their ignorance of hers. In this instance, she's intrigued by Champlain's open face and good manners, not the usual greedy trader, and that he carries no weapons, leaving his Swiss mercenaries in the bay. A man, she concludes, familiar with the art of befriending strangers. It's no reason to let her guard down but in the spirit of diplomatic pragmatism, she invites him ashore to learn more about his mission and whether he's likely to be a danger to her clan.

They enter the clearing on the valley floor, finding themselves encircled by wigwams. With a nod from Muin'iskw, the Mi'kmaq men and women disperse, now certain this isn't a bartering session. They've learned from experience when it's time to bring out the pelts hidden in the woods. This is not that time. Reading the evolving situation quickly, Champlain directs his own men back to the beach.

"This is a beautiful land," Champlain says earnestly.

"Our people from the time long before spoke of this valley as a world of ice," Muin'iskw says. "Ice in all seasons, ice everywhere. Gods of ice that swam through this river to die in the great sea."

"A world of ice," Champlain says, confused. "Gods..."

As the fog reasserts itself, Muin'iskw leads them toward the house, which they approach through the back garden where nothing visible has emerged yet other than a patch of rhubarb.

"Your home appears of pleasing character," Champlain says.

"It is where we welcome honored visitors," she says.

"And this building is of your making, Poirier?"

In a feverish stream of French, Basque, and Mi'kmaq, Poirier talks about the site of the house, chosen after much experimentation, built among the wigwams but slightly apart, a protected space sculpted within the trees, open to the sun, but fencing in gardens front and back, away from the communal fire. As Poirier continues, Champlain at times struggles to follow him. To him, the man sounds like he's reciting a prayer, or speaking to a spirit force, to a god if not the Christian God.

"Poirier, you have done honor for yourself with your home."

"It is not my home for my family," comes the reply, a sadness in his voice. "It is the home of our people. A home we all share."

Champlain is confused: "So perhaps it is your Church now?"

Poirier gives him a skeptical look.

"It is God's blessing to live here," Champlain says obliviously as he wanders into the garden along a meandering stone path. Meanwhile Muin'iskw continues on and enters the house alone.

The stones along the path are all etched in drawings, mostly animal imagery, caribou and moose, but others are stranger, monstrous hybrids, a water serpent with a leering smile. There are humans in

78

many scenes, stick figures, some in canoes, others on the hunt, some forlornly alone, thin arms raised to the sky as if giving praise or in submission to unseen forces. It is overwhelming to Champlain.

"Are these the accomplishments of your wife?"

Poirier just smiles. "We should go inside."

Inside Champlain confronts a low-ceilinged room with a central hearth that is alive with fire, a wall of carpentry tools and a long wooden table in one corner but no other signs of domesticity.

"I see tools of your craft never seen before in France."

"I made them, here, to help with the needs of my people."

"*My* people," Muin'iskw says, mischievous, pride in her voice, leading Champlain to the table where a young woman, just leaving, has set down three steaming bowls of chowder

"This is a robust abode," Champlain says.

The structure is a variation on *piece sur piece* construction, the walls made with logs compressed one on top the other, the gaps between each filled with seaweed then covered with birch bark."

"Poirier, where did you acquire such expertise?"

"I lived among masons and builders for a time."

"And yet here you are."

Poirier pauses, clears his throat, then. "My father. Like many he fought for your King and died in battle. I was orphaned at fourteen."

"The wars have taken many good men from us."

"I too was a soldier. What I have seen. The killing. Because of a difference in thinking about the same God? That is the Devil's work!"

Champlain is nonplussed by the outburst from Poirier who retreats into himself, embarrassed.

"I can understand why the wars inspired you to build a life here, Poirier, away from hate."

Muin'iskw says, calmly, in French, "Do you believe it possible that your world of hate will not descend upon us here?"

Champlain is briefly taken aback by her directness, then: "There is hate all over the world. It is not unknown here, even among your people."

"Our people have ways of settling our differences, honorably."

"You speak of a legitimate concern but you have my word, our intent is partnership, to establish relations of mutual benefit."

"Your words," she replies caustically. "And the Word of your God? Our people throughout this land—those who have parleyed with those from your world—do not believe your words yet. They hear many words, but we can agree that words have their limits."

"I am only one man. I can only speak for my intentions."

"Do you speak for the men and guns on your ship?"

Champlain grimaces but says no more, as there is nothing more to say, not now, he realizes. Diplomacy is a journey that takes time.

As they eat in uncomfortable silence, Champlain covertly studies Poirier, thinking about the mystery of the man, his strange eloquence for things most do not notice about the spaces in which they live. For an orphan, Poirier is too well educated, so articulate. And arriving here on a whaler from San Sebastian seems farfetched. There must be lies here, some manipulation of truth. While he's sorting out how to question Poirier further, he looks up to see Muin'iskw studying him, and feels her probing intelligence drowning the space between them.

They're interrupted by a commotion: men shouting.

They rush outside to see one of Champlain's men and a Mi'kmaq man in a fist fight near the dunes, their comrades cheering each man on. As he runs toward the fight, Champlain is overtaken by Muin'iskw, her husband a stride behind. As Champlain follows, a few steps behind, he watches as Muin'iskw launches herself between the two men, breaking them apart. The situation is tense. Insults and taunts keep flying between the opposing sides, the clamor of men nearly unhinged.

Champlain wades in, angrily instructing his men to retreat to the skiffs. Meanwhile, Muin'iskw admonishes the Mi'kmaq men.

"I must apologize for the behavior of my men," Champlain says gravely to Muin'iskw. "They have been at sea for too long and are unused to the ways of this world, yet. I am to blame."

Muin'iskw turns to Champlain, and in French says, "We have been poor hosts. Our younger men have been taught better."

Champlain nods, but doesn't feel fully himself, either, realizing he too is suffering the effects of being on the sea for weeks.

The exchange of apologies continues, as Champlain and Muin'iskw attempt to outdo the other in accepting responsibility for the fight that was verging on becoming much more violent.

"Muin'iskw, in taking my leave I must compliment you on your artistry in your garden," Champlain says, edging into the shallows. "I will study your drawings one day if you will allow it."

"We shall see what the future brings," she replies, calmly.

Champlain's men, some openly grumbling, are crammed again into their skiffs. The Mi'kmaq men and women behind Muin'iskw want to return to what they were doing but can't until the Europeans leave.

Everyone's eager for this moment to end.

* * *

Hours later, at sunset, Champlain works at a table in the officer's quarters on the ship, sketching the outlines of a map based on the measurements taken and the calculations made that day.

Pierre Dugua, the expedition commander, sits opposite him, writing in his diary, periodically refilling their wine cups.

"Champlain. This camp?"

"What we anticipated. Seasonal. The fish trade mainly."

"And the Frenchman there. His provenance?"

"He spoke some French. I detected the flavor of La Rochelle, or Saintonge at any rate. But curiously he claimed to be from the Pyrenees, from Navarre, not quite French, not quite Spanish."

"Indeed, our Basque friends are notoriously...independent. The mountains will do that to a man. Difficult people."

"Perhaps, he was transported here, after being been given the choice of confinement—or death—in a French prison. Or perhaps he was forcefully employed on a fishing vessel. If not a Basque whaler. Perhaps his freedom was purchased by the owner of one such ship? Perhaps he escaped this ship, hid in the forest, before his debt to the owner was cleared. How he arrived here, it is for God to answer."

They work in silence for a while.

"Champlain, for your map, shall we indulge in naming this place to honor our King? This is your area of expertise, after all."

"Indeed, naming is a way of—"

"Asserting ownership, among other things."

"This is not the thought that always dominates my thinking."

Dugua laughs. "You are a more enlightened man than I."

"Cap de la Hève."

"Perfect! The last of land we saw in leaving France."

"And it is a haven for the people here. Their safe haven."

* * *

At dusk, carving a stone drawing, Muin'iskw sits alone on the platform on the drumlin ridge.

As the sunset tints the sky a vibrant rose, she pauses to gaze at the horizon. Everything's so still right now.

She trusts no one about the future.

She swivels to face the mouth of the estuary where the French ship on the opposite shore now begins to head out to sea again.

In the quiet of the evening, she hears a hammering noise, then her husband's voice, laughing, instructing other men—

What is he building now?

He will build until he dies, he thinks. And if they burn what he builds, he will build again. For that is his purpose.

The etching she's working on is a circle that contains an eight-pointed star, her way of paying respects to the Great Spirit who comes to her when she least expects it.

And now for the first time in years...she recalls her etching of the warrior helmet and its white feather.

She now knows how to etch the face.

December 1620

They tell each other they aren't hiding but doing as they have done every year, returning to the forest upriver and settling in for the winter.

The question neither asks: what choice did we have?

All through the fall, as the storms came and went, and others in the clan left not just because of the season but because of the danger, he worked to repair the walls and roof from the attack in the summer. It was the house he had built for her and he wouldn't leave until he was done. Their son helped him while she prepared the canoes for the journey and then hid the rest of their things in the woods. Their daughter and her husband had left weeks before.

One morning the husband came back and told them another attack was imminent. It really was time to leave and so they did.

Over the winter they both talked hopefully about going back in the spring, as they did every year. But when the storyteller appeared at the oval wigwam, a figure dusted in snow, his beard icicled, he told them about the men and the weapons who had arrived in their absence and how they had cleared all the land and built new structures.

He said they should never go back there except in their dreams.

October 1689

Under the lean-to on the drumlin ridge, she watches it unfold, cozy under blankets, clutching a doll made of rags and straw. She was asleep when awakened by the flames roaring in the darkness, fascinated as only a child can be by something sad yet thrilling.

The solitary house in the field below had been dying for years. Trading at the camp had declined because of competition from the Acadian settlements on Baie Francaise. In the winter, no one came here except for Mi'kmaq hunting parties venturing too far from home. The good timber had long been turned into firewood or stolen by the few traders who still worked this coastline, including her own parents. The last residents were a family of raccoons.

All that remained when they arrived this year was a cluster of rotten beams piled on top of the stone hearth in the granite cellar that had begun to tumble inward from pressure exerted by thawing land in the spring. They told her today that this will be the last season here, given how poor the trading was. In a week from now, Beausoleil will return with the ship and take them back to Grand-Pre for the winter.

She cried when she arrived this year and discovered that someone had dug up and taken the stone drawings in the old garden.

She wonders how the fire started. All her father said before heading down the hill was that tomorrow morning, after the burning stops, they'll scavenge in the ashes for every last nail, which they'll take back for repairs on their house and the dykes around their farm.

Tonight the abandoned skeleton of the house is an inferno etched against the night. The thought she has while falling asleep is that the house, this ghost of fire, is the most beautiful thing she's ever seen.

February 1779

The man carrying an axe trudges up the trail toward the woods, burdened by thoughts he'd rather not have.

83

He's mindful enough to pick his spots in navigating the ice, the fingers of marbled whiteness here and there on browned land, now sweating in surface melt. It's an unusually mild and sunny winter morning, a thaw on. Even now, only an hour past dawn, water drip-drips from the outbuildings and puddles up the barnyard mud.

His father has been dead six days, but the land is too hard with frost to bury him. They've been forced to improvise, hauling the body up to the loft of the barn. His wife, heavily pregnant, declared she won't go in there for chores. Neither will anyone else. No one wants an unblessed corpse lying around. What choice is there? The minister might arrive on the next boat or ox cart, but that could be weeks away. He thinks about carrying his father to the top of the hill and setting him ablaze on a mound of hemlock as the sun drops from the sky. He doesn't know where the thought comes from but knows it's a sin.

The dampness under the clear skies and in the breeze suggests more rain tonight that will turn to ice by morning. He looks back at his house, what today we'd call a Cape, built a generation back, featuring double-hung sash windows, Georgian style, around the perimeter and a central chimney mass that warms rooms on two floors.

84

He's thirty, ruggedly lean, not yet starting to hunch in the way of men who push their bodies too hard working the fields and the sea. As a younger man before returning to the village to marry his second cousin, he'd spent three years on the Grand Banks off Newfoundland, jigging cod from dawn to dusk, bobbing up and down in a small dory on the mountainous seas. At the time he didn't think the work was dangerous but on mornings like this, as he walks up the hill toward the woods, and pauses now and then to take in the ocean horizon from the elevated height, he speaks to God, thanking Him for bringing him home alive, for giving him a family in this isolated paradise.

Today his optimism is nowhere active in him. In the ambiguous looks of his neighbors offering condolences, he senses blame for allowing his father to die before the ground thawed. To make matters worse, he has finally accepted this morning that he will have to kill and butcher the older of his two oxen, the one named Bright, his steadfast companion for years on the farm. His wife was very clear: Bright's time had come. The ox will have to be killed and slow cooked for a family meal, with generous portions shared in the village. And he's just not sure he, himself, can eat an old friend he shared so much with.

He's a farmer from one of the founding families in the village. They were "foreign Protestants" who came to Lunenburg County in the early 1750s from northwest Switzerland and southwest Germany. At the invitation of the British authorities, keen to settle territory won from the French but still very much violently disputed by the Mi'kmaq, these German-speaking immigrants were fleeing the hardships of political fragmentation in Europe after the Roman Empire collapsed. The continent was at war arising from religious extremism and the struggle for survival among hundreds of microstates. Of the many thousands of Protestant immigrants to North America, some three thousand came to Nova Scotia, including this man's parents and their kin. He remembers nothing of his early childhood in Switzerland, other than a recurring sense of anxiety still resident in him about being in bumpy motion for what was an eternity to a young boy, the weeks and months in transit, in the stagecoach that took them to Rotterdam from Bern, then in the deep bowels of the ship that crossed the sea, and then, after three soggy, impoverished winters in Halifax, being seasick on the sail to Lunenburg and onwards again in the ox cart to where he lives now.

He enters the woods for a day of harvesting hardwood that he needs to make a new batch of tools for the coming farm season. He wouldn't admit it to anyone, but the aroma and stillness of the winter forest is his incense, a mysterious and sacred force. A few times a year, in Lunenburg, he'll get into a real church after the trading is done and while the oxen rest up for the long cart-ride home. It doesn't compare with being alone here. Some days, on the way in, he'll sit down on the big mossy boulder for reasons never clear to him. But something demands that thoughtless pause to survey the iced-up forest floor etched in pine needles, his gaze occasionally veering up into sunlight that penetrates the canopy of trees in thin slivers. Sometimes, he'll recite a bible passage, usually in German. But after they got a King James version, he began comparing passages in both languages and now recites in English to improve his facility in his second language.

Needing his spirits lifted, he whispers out a memorized passage:

And all these blessings shall come upon you and overtake you, if you obey the voice of the Lord your God. Blessed shall you be in the city and blessed shall you be in the field. Blessed shall be the fruit of your womb and the

*fruit of your ground and the fruit of your cattle, the increase of your herds
and the young of your flock.*

Blessed he might be by the God in Heaven, but it was a winter
from Hell, one storm after another, as his father lay dying in the small
room behind the kitchen, the borning room, unable to sit up in his
last week. They took turns sitting with him through his dying. He'd
given up English, speaking only German while sucking on an unlit
pipe and drifting through a lifetime of memories. Over and over the
rebellion came up, the time they all went into Lunenburg with pitch-
forks and hammers, threatening to take on the local colonial bosses
for not providing the provisions or the livestock they promised them
in cultivating their lands. He was proud he'd been arrested, locked up
for weeks, but their demands were ultimately met, affirming him as a
leader in the village.

A man, his son thinks, people could trust.

As he works alone butchering a fallen oak, he reflects on what his
father taught him, and at times is shocked to find his face wet with
tears, his vision so clouded he often stops to regain his composure.

There has been no crying to this point, no open displays of grief
but dour acceptance, and the need for responsibility, doing the right
thing because that's what you do when you don't have the luxury of
expressing certain emotions around others who count on you to be
strong. So here, among the trees he compromises the only way he mor-
ally knows how: grieving while being productive, thinking ahead to the
spring, the tools needed, crying alone, hour after hour, and wondering
if his father had ever cried in front of others—or ever.

He thinks of the time when the man from town, the bigshot owner
of three fishing schooners, showed up with an offer to buy all the hardwood they could cut, and was astonished by the house his father had
built over the old foundations and that was now his house.

"What style of house is that, sir," the man asked. "It is very pleasing
in its proportions."

"It is the house you build when you cannot afford any other house.
A house where you cannot afford errors in the making."

"You have learned well the craft of building, sir."

"There is much to learn and little to teach about the craft of building, but what can be taught can be taught clearly."

He thinks of his father's stern gaze when he said he wanted to buy new windows for his fish shack on the shore.

"Vanity is a vice in the eyes of God."

His son still has trouble with his father's severity. Would I not work harder with more light to guide me? Would I not spend more time inside at work the more pleasant my views? They finally agreed to compromise: when the windows on the house needed replacing, they could be recycled in the fish shack.

Years away, he thinks ruefully.

He thinks of the time before he married, a Saturday night when he and his cousins, all of them young men, sat around the barn with a jug of bootleg rum, his father walking in, saying nothing but of course he didn't have to, ending everything instantly.

He thinks of his father staring him down when he threatened to leave once and for all and make his fortune somewhere else, not here where the only pleasures were taken in work, in prayer, in sacrifice.

"Whether you leave or stay, don't be one of those people who waste their lives criticizing," his father said. "Make something better."

Have I made something better, he wonders, as he stumbles through the woods toward the valley, dead tired, chilled now, the sweat congealing on his undershirt as the temperature drops, a fact he neglects to notice until now. Coming out onto the ridge, the valley bright with late-afternoon sun, he confronts his youngest son.

"Papa, come now."

"What is it?"

"Mama is in the borning room."

So her time is here. Another child, God willing.

Have I made something better?

He starts running—

Six hours from now, his second son will be born healthy.

What he doesn't know is that wife will be dead in two years and that he will remarry again and they will have three more children here.

And when his time comes, he too will retire to the borning room as a village elder held in high esteem as his father once was, and allow himself to die there, his destiny in God's hands. But in this moment, as he runs toward the house, he is flush with the energy of believing paradise isn't just dreamed but birthed one moment at a time.

July 1972

The old house has survived so much: the storms of a volatile climate, the looters, the summertime play of children from the village over the hill who conjure ghosts while playing Cowboys-and-Indians, marauding teenagers getting drunk, or pregnant. It has thrived as a sentinel of lonely endurance while every other building here turned to empty footprint, to broken outlines of stone. It has a solemn dignity that speaks to a bygone community once cultivated with great care, unlike the unkempt fields and scrub forest that now surround it. It has survived so much and still seems immortal to the few who come over the hill in good weather to go fishing in the morning. It feels so permanent that it's almost invisible, something you don't notice in its unchanging quiet. Then comes the airborne trail of burning ash—the burning essence of something—that escapes upwards from the metal drum over the hill where they're incinerating trash on a theoretically windless day. And suddenly the old house again abandons its physicality, turns into fire and light, into absence and charred ruin.

April 1983

"Look at that," Brian says, voice booming, steps ahead of Marilyn as they walk down the hill toward the valley and the cliffs fronting on the estuary. It's a day like many here, constantly shifting in mood. Impossible to predict one minute to the next whether to layer up or down. In the softness of the afternoon light, it's colder than it looks, which they discover as they meander closer to the shore.

"Brian, slow down a little," she says

She sounds more impatient than she is. Still, she won't rush into manic lockstep. She feels an obligation at times to fuse his boundless energy—much like they fused their last names into hyphenated form, hers MacKay, his Lyons—with her calmer sense of pace. She doesn't really want him to slow down. She just wants to move at her own speed. If there's any tension in the moment for her, it doesn't meet the test of conflict suppressed for the sake of domestic harmony. This is just another new adventure—or experiment—in their young marriage where the work is very much about trying to establish an equilibrium between her enthusiasms and his.

They're well matched by the looks of things. Each has a wide strong face, hers with piercing green eyes, his piercing blue. Both have a measured way of speaking with voices that carry some authority in seminar rooms but have a more relaxed or colloquial energy with friends around a dinner table or bonfire. There are clues that they're white-collared, multi-degree professionals: his Yankees ball cap and moleskin notebook, her Frye boots and acid-washed jeans. The broad contours of their dreams for a life together are sketched out, although the practical realities are still sketchy. There's alignment on the big questions—like starting a family—but so much else is unknown.

"It's something, right?" he says, talking to himself, involuntarily on the move towards what he's not yet sure.

Like her husband, she sees everything available to the senses in the experience here of landscape and sea, the hill and the valley, the trees and the fields, the sky and what's under it, the horizon in the distance, the soggy field after heavy rain. She sees the beauty and power in all the dynamics of the scene. After all, she's a pattern-seeking scientist working towards her PhD.

"Over here," he says, from the valley floor.

Her curiosity rises with what's surging through him in each purposeful stride as he ploughs ahead, sometimes through cow patties she elects to dodge. Years later, he'll say, we were looking for a home, I guess, and the area felt like the place I grew up. But there was something else speaking to him that day, when they found the old foundation. He knew then if he followed the message of the ruins, he could live one kind of life. It was a test of something.

They vaguely knew the area when they bought the old Cape Cod house in the village last week. After the woman, a village elder, accepted their offer, written out on the back of an envelope and finalized over tea in her kitchen, Brian and Marilyn walked giddily up the road toward the coast. Through a few despondent strands of third-growth forest, they emerged in the valley to see what locals call the Back Shore. There wasn't time for a thorough investigation of what was over there, other than knowing it had been cow pasture. They were a little disoriented, having arguably made the most imprudent decision since getting married: buying a rural property before settling into a home in Halifax where they both have teaching positions. His father thought they were nuts. Hers loved the idea but was an incorrigible risk-taker himself, always doubling down on everything in his many business ventures back in PEI.

And now Brian stands before the ruins of the old house in the valley, hands on his hips, head swiveling, a leg up on a corroded granite block that appears to have bled iron in its long life. The ruins are just a rubble pit now, overgrown in daffodils, rhubarb, ferns. Mosses and fungi smear the foundation and the rotted timber strewn throughout. There are modest signs of careless human interference, a broken lobster trap, a grouping of gutted aerosol cans, a waterlogged beer case emptied of bottles, and the feathered skeleton of a seagull.

Marilyn saunters away from the ruins and learns there are more foundations in the valley, and considerable evidence of previous habitation: multiple building footprints of all sizes, abandoned wells, and fence lines stitching the landscape, some barely visible in the overgrowth. She imagines an entire village here. And today, she thinks, it's nothing but neglected history, a world forgetting itself one day at a time on land most would consider worthless. She looks back to where Brian should be standing and now isn't. He's jumped into the ruins, only the back of his head visible to her right now.

"Marilyn, you need to see this."

Words that have given her pause before and will again.

When she approaches, he starts to gesture, illustrating the contours of the massive basement hearth that has mostly collapsed into a heap of stone within the outline of the foundation walls of the perimeter. "Even like this, it feels primal, monumental."

"I wonder what the house looked like. Who lived here?"

"I guarantee it looked a lot like our Cape. Built like a ship."

"It's a pretty exposed place to build, Brian," she says, looking around, raising her voice above the echoes of surf. "Would you want to live out here. Hard to imagine it."

He stands there, wordlessly absorbed.

She instantly sees a future here: these ruins have a vital hold on him, and consequently, it will have a hold on *them*. One day, when the land here comes up for sale, they'll make another imprudent decision and take on debt to buy it.

For years to come, he'll talk of this moment as an epiphany, a crucial plot point that spins his life and work forward in synch.

What he confronts in the collapsed hearth inside the womb of the ancient foundation is, for him, the ultimate symbol for family, the centre of everything. In its sublime neglect, he finds a source of inspiration to build his practice around and, very soon, inspire the renovation of the Cape Cod house they just bought. In this landscape, he will reframe the meaning of architectural originality as a return to origins, where tradition and modernity are meaningless distinctions. This just isn't a ruined house to him. It had once been a temple for living, he'll say to his students, paraphrasing Louis Kahn, an expression of optimism by people who had only themselves to rely on. He'll talk about the hearth as a Jungian archetype, a *totem* that will figure into the grammar of his work for decades. He will generate from these ruins a theory about the architectural values of ordinary vernacular buildings and relate that to the perspective that greatness in so many classic art forms derives from folk traditions, and from lives of hardship and poverty, much like those who once lived and died in this valley.

"This was Indian habitation here," he says abruptly.

"Brian."

"I mean Native—or First Nations. Aboriginal. The language keeps changing...I mean no disrespect."

In the car driving back to Halifax, she gets him to promise that they'll enjoy the Cape in the shape it's currently in. There's no money to renovate right now, she says. We're all tapped out, Brian.

Next weekend they're back in the Cape Cod again. It's Brian and Marilyn and a few friends with crowbars, tearing out walls and floors, everyone coated in dust and horsehair insulation from the original build. Soon enough all the rooms are gone and so is the second floor. What's left is an exoskeleton, the exterior walls into which Brian will design a massive hearth-like form that tapers up through the centre of the house, emerging from the roof as a cedar-shingled lookout. He will graft a lighthouse into the emptied guts of a farmhouse. At the bottom of the form, a stone fireplace will define the main floor but, as it rises up higher, two sleeping lofts will peel off from the chimney core, drawbridge-style. He names it House on the Nova Scotia Coast #1. It wins prestigious awards and announces his intention as an architect. More personally: it's his way of following the message of the ruins he discovered with Marilyn on the Back Shore.

In the small narrow field behind the house, he plants an apple orchard, introducing another archetype into the scheme, the grove. He doesn't want the land to exist as merely something to look at. He wants it to work. He won't be a tourist but a builder of his adopted community. And so he will spend weekends and vacations here for years, too often in the rain, boot-deep in mud, planting trees, trying to protect them from the deer, and failing over and over. He'll work to exhaustion, dawn to dusk, in all seasons, planting and replanting trees, a local Sisyphus, providing entertainment for the few remaining farmers here who are amused and impressed. Some neighbors will become cherished friends, often feeding Brian and Marilyn with chowder and biscuits, a pot of tea, and pep talks when things don't go so well for the young couple, which is only to be expected. They quickly become integral to the community and for Brian and Marilyn it does feel like a homecoming.

These are exciting years when they are both doing too much. It's not enough to teach and reach for tenure, he must actively practice as an architect. But in their economically depressed city, Halifax, mired in a deep recession, there's little enthusiasm for architectural utopianism coming from someone still wet behind the ears, still in his twenties. *Who does he think he is? The nerve! The ego!* He runs into a classic Maritime psychological vice, the residue of colonialism or provincialism: looking down on anyone who openly wants to better himself and take matters into his or her own hands. But he puts his shingle out there anyway, renovating a former gas station in a rougher part of town for his tiny firm, hires people, and starts to win commissions. He designs a few houses for people in the Kingsburg area, the self-described village architect, while undertaking small developments in Halifax that test the narrow tolerances of a retrograde zoning regime. But making little money. As we enter the 1990s, suddenly children are arriving, but they can't afford for either parent to stay home. There are times when it's Marilyn's salary that not only puts food on the table but keeps his practice afloat.

During this period, a hidden chamber constructs itself in Brian's psychology that won't make itself fully known or even affect him much for years, although it eventually does. This is where he will store the guilt for what he puts Marilyn and their family through pursuing his dreams as an architect. But in these early years of family life and in his practice, neither will dwell much on the costs, the sacrifices, not only because there's always too much to do, but because everything's worth it. What they're building, they're building together.

For years, on weekend mornings, after acquiring the land in the valley, he will walk there from the village with his dog, regardless of the weather, to clear trees with a chainsaw, priming it for cultivation and his building projects. As time passes, the ingredients of a promise to himself start mixing within him, although it takes years for the promise to become words he shares with others, which is this: that whatever he builds in this valley will speak to the Métis sensibility he admires so much for its communal spirit and respect for nature.

On his own among the ruins there are no limits to what's possible.

4
SkyRoom II

SLOUCHED IN THE HIGH-BACKED ADIRONDACK chair I'm brought to my senses by the snowflakes wafting down out of the darkness into the floodlit quietness of the SkyRoom. But nothing yet is landing intact, no smudges of fragile whiteness coagulating on anything. It reminds me of a phrase we all learned as kids watching the space missions on TV: *burning up on re-entry*. These fat snowflakes are burning up before I'm even tempted to stick out my tongue to catch one. For an instant they're floating into my field of vision, then they vanish, although there's a sensation of droplets tickling my forehead, a subtle feeling of being swarmed, or disturbed, even if gently so, from the weeping sky.

How long have I been here?

Boots crunching on hard-packed snow—

The howling wind is above ground, not on me, not down here.

And then there's Brian coming down the granite steps, a wine bottle in hand, followed by Marilyn, outfitted in dark workout gear under a grey shawl, a black laptop case at her side.

It's bright enough down here with the floodlights on, but, even so, it's cold, my breath visible, the impulse strong to cup my palms and loudly blow into them.

Brian pours us each a glass as Marilyn sits down opposite me, taking out a gleaming silver laptop while stretching her legs out to a footstool. It's stopped snowing but the snowflakes have flecked her shawl, leggings and long dark hair. I get a smile from her and a few questions about the wellbeing of my family, then she's down to work on a lecture she's giving in Halifax where she's a full professor at Dalhousie and runs a research laboratory that applies physiotherapy principles to the recovery of stroke survivors.

"So this is Marilyn's favorite place at Shobac," I say, nodding to Brian, wondering whether Marilyn will multi-task into the conversation.

"Tell him a little about Stew," she says, between clicks, producing a warm but momentary smile. "That might explain a few things about why we ended up together and here, Brian."

So Brian launches into backstory about Marilyn's father, Stew MacKay, apparently a legend as a serial entrepreneur on Prince Edward Island where Marilyn grew up in Charlottetown, the provincial capital. After quitting school at twelve to support his family, Stew went on to start dozens of businesses over a lifetime. He was into everything, real estate, furniture, potato and fox farming, tourism, a string of grocery stores, a cheese factory, a butcher shop, a laundromat, auto supplies. He introduced architecture into Marilyn's life. On a trip to Newfoundland, he saw a house that looked, as Brian puts it, "like some circular amoeba house out of German Expressionism, or the Jetsons." Stew finds out who the architect is, buys the plans, and builds the exact same house back home, complete with vertical pink and green-striped siding and plastic bubble skylights.

"Stew could and would sell anything, let me tell you" Brian says. "One time Marilyn came home and there was an old house in the driveway, up on blocks. Why he did that I don't—"

"I don't quite remember it that way," Marilyn says slowly over a languorous flow of laptop clicks. "I don't think the house was actually in our driveway. I'm not sure where it was."

Brian revectors the story without missing a beat and relates how Marilyn's mother came home one day to discover all her furniture outside, replaced with Modernist classics, a Noguchi table, Eames chair and ottoman, Aalto chairs, a lava lamp. Stew decided the new stuff would work better with the Jetsons-amoeba house. Brian tells a few more stories about Marilyn's father, a man following dreams, heedless of consequence or what others might think, an autodidact, too, a bottomless appetite for educating himself about the world.

Brian's watching me, waiting for the light bulb to go off in my head, then decides to turn it on for me.

"Stew was crazier than I am—of that I'm pretty certain—but there's a case to be made here that Marilyn married her father."

Marilyn, still clicking away, is nonplussed by the assertion, and while still looking at her screen, says, "Well, there was the time we came home and there were forty or fifty white fridges lined up in the yard. Like some kind of appliance graveyard."

I burst out laughing.

She turns to me, blinks once, then twice, giving nothing more away, then goes back to her screen, then adds. "Stew was a mentor to

Brian in an important way, I'd say. For us both. He certainly taught us that in life you could and need to take risks to get anywhere. And if anything, Larry, this place has been a journey in risk. Still is."

Given her matter-of-fact tone, gentle as it is, she's clearly speaking to Brian. A conversation that doubtless started a long time ago.

"As for my motivations about Shobac," she continues in a shoulder-shrugging way. "At first I didn't pay attention or maybe I was just blind. But it soon became clear he was building things here that were really going to stress us, financially."

She gives me a look clouded enough to suggest their utopia here did not spring fully realized out of a fairy tale. I mean, how could it? I'm thinking, there's unvarnished ambition in everything around their situation at Shobac. How could it not come at high personal or financial cost? The sheepish look on Brian's face confirms it. I sense the tension between them right now, not as a clear and present danger to the moment, as something likely to erupt, but as an old friend in their relationship they're careful not to summon—around me at least—in anything but oblique generalities as I probe into their lives here.

What they concede is that over the years a pattern established itself as Brian forged ahead with bigger building projects at Shobac that each time apparently laid a surprise at Marilyn's feet, some with difficult financial implications. Problem is, I don't buy that Marilyn could ever be consistently fooled by anyone. I suggest to her that she likes being surprised, anticipates it, has an appetite for the unpredictability and risks that Brian introduces into their lives. Just like her father did. In the pause before she answers, I can virtually see her mind sorting and shaping all the possible responses, as if weighing them against an honesty standard. To my knowledge she isn't a person who, as a primary impulse, stretches the boundaries of her own truth.

"I'm not sure my mind works that way," she says, humbly. "My father was a man of surprises, good ones mostly. And what we have here, as hard as it has been at times, has been a wonderful journey."

I've shaken something loose in Marilyn, and on she goes, telling a story about a vacation at the family cottage when she was in her teens.

She and her siblings and their mother, all sun-drunk from a day at the beach, and wrapped in colorful beach towels, had just walked back to the cottage as a gorgeous sunset melted upon them.

And there was Stew at the grill, doing burgers.

Up until that moment it had been the perfect vacation. Day four. Ten more to go. Each evening after cleanup, there were card and board games, Scrabble, Monopoly. Then everyone to bed before eleven, and up early for pancakes, then another day in the sun and water.

Then Stew announced, after a burger-flipping flourish, that they would have to cut things short in three more days, truncating the holiday by a week. He'd just rented the cottage to another family

Shocking everyone, but perhaps not his wife.

"He didn't lack empathy," Marilyn says, "But he looked at us and said, 'You all want to go to college?' And of course we were all stunned silent. And then he said, 'So where's the money coming from?'"

The question hangs visibly in the air.

It's easy to imagine Marilyn as the super-active mother and grandmother, frequently there to babysit or read bedtime stories.

Also easy to imagine her as a professional at work, making things happen according to the business plan. She's the stable, sensible and sane person, never one to run from the less glorious tasks, like cleaning the bathroom drains in a rental cabin or sorting the garbage because it wasn't done right in the first place.

What's harder to imagine is Marilyn as a persistent risk-taker, embracing financial ambiguity and constant disruptions as she's done with Brian over so many years in turning Shobac into what it is today. But in Stew MacKay's daughter, it seems, the fever of entrepreneurialism also burns unchecked, making her an ideal partner for the adventures in utopian and architectural possibility that make Shobac her accomplishment as much as it is Brian's.

They've built Shobac in the context of a delicate collectivity, their family. Their son Matt, the youngest sibling at thirty-one, is an architect in Brian's practice. Brian tells me Matt wanted to be an architect, much like himself, also at an absurdly early age, six. He delights in telling me that the boy said he wanted to follow his father's path "because all architects do is travel and talk to people."

"Some truth in that."

"Guilty as charged."

The middle child, Ali, a veterinarian, was first to join her parents in making a life at Shobac. She oversees the breeding practices of the farm animals and offers horse-riding lessons to visitors.

Their firstborn child, Renée, is a structural engineer who recently moved back to Nova Scotia with her husband Peter, a lawyer. She's taken an office in her father's studio in town, working remotely for a Toronto engineering firm. She collaborates today on projects with Brian's firm. "When Renée was very young, I'd pick her up at school and we'd go to lunch and come back to my studio, where we'd set her up with crayons and paper. I remember her saying, 'I always do my best work in my Dad's office.' Amazing how life repeats itself at times."

As we talk, the snow starts to fall again, so Marilyn packs her laptop away in its case. There's a well-tempered deference between my friends, each generous in allowing the other conversational airtime, perhaps not an unusual quality in a long-married couple. Neither strives to talk over the other. But their duet showcases much different styles. Brian is the seasoned raconteur with well-traveled anecdotes that he spices in humorous exaggeration and punchline twists. Marilyn is more open-ended, less premeditated, more likely to figure out what she's saying in the moment she's saying it, but with a lawyer's gift for parsing the differentiating nuance or mitigating circumstance. Taciturn, empathetic, but formidable. Do not take her lightly in a field-hockey or basketball game—two sports she excelled at in school. You'll end up on your butt. If you try to put one over on her, you'll pay. As a college student walking home through a park late one night, she not only convinced a gang of thugs not to rob her, but to reach into their pockets and give her some money before sending her on her way, unharmed.

Brian and Marilyn are equal partners in the Shobac enterprise, theirs being a marriage born out of first-wave feminism. This is and always has been a two-career marriage—or three, if you include Shobac. And yet, their quest for marital equality has been achieved by navigating the occasional deviation from the feminist playbook.

Marilyn's mother, a cultured, independent woman, was a country schoolteacher before becoming a nurse. She had strongly encouraged her daughters from the start to be even more independent and career-driven than she was, not a slave to domesticity. On Marilyn and Brian's wedding day, however, she cornered the bride minutes before the ceremony and made her swear on the Bible that she wouldn't do anything to compromise Brian in his calling as an architect.

Marilyn swore.

When it came time for Marilyn to choose a career after getting her undergraduate degree, she sat down with her parents and siblings and said she was applying to physiotherapy school, not medical school. She tells me, "When I said that you could hear a pin drop around the table, until one of my sisters more or less shouted, 'how pedestrian!'"

Her mother was outraged that Marilyn, who had the marks to get into medical school, was giving up on her childhood dream of becoming a brain surgeon.

"She should have gotten you to swear on the Bible about going to medical school," I say, getting an uneasy laugh.

"It was a calculation," she replies evenly. "I was involved with a complicated guy, and really wanted to have a family, several kids, and a career helping people. That was the criteria, the situation. But something had to give. I didn't become a surgeon, true, but I have made a career helping people with their health. I wanted it all but it had to be all, not missing parts, and that took some thinking."

"How much of a sacrifice?"

She looks at me in a way suggesting that sacrifice is a much longer subject than we have time for. "There is so much I get here, being with family, in this landscape, where what Brian's created has been handled with so much sensitivity," she offers in a way that doesn't invite doubt. "I don't get the visceral thrill of designing and building like Brian does, but we're all-in here, both of us, each with our role."

"So, how would you define your role?"

"I'm the enabler!" she says, laughing.

The snow has really started to fall. Before much more is said, Brian and Marilyn are up on their feet, dusting snow from themselves and telling me it's time for them to call it a night. Then they're gone.

For years I've watched Shobac evolve as Brian and Marilyn unified their lives there. I'm envious about what I'm still struggling to achieve myself since getting married thirty years ago and starting a family with Alison. Our lives are rewarding and frankly privileged, thanks to careers that make good things possible for a family of four and a succession of tabby cats. But we've moved around so much because of me, my inability to *settle*. For the longest time we lived in a city far from here where the record shows we've visited Nova Scotia about three months a year for some twenty years. In the city, we've moved ten times in our

102

lives there. These days, as empty nesters, we're here more, almost full time, given that our two boys are now out of the house, creating their own lives.

Why have I been more nomadic than has been good for our family?

Why do I still feel rootless at times or *misplaced*?

The Shobac dream that Brian and Marilyn have brought to life doesn't answer these questions, but it triggers something unresolved, an ache for full-on domestic integration in one place.

Snow falling through fog on a blackened night is the strangest thing. Disorienting in a good way. Especially being surrounded as I am by all this granite so eloquently assembled. It generates in me the loopy illusion that I'm capable right now of speaking to the deities that control the spasms of meteorological complexity now blinding me.

I wish I could sit here all night, caked in snow, falling off to sleep with my feet warmed by a small fire struggling for life.

5
Ghost Stories

SKYROOM   LARRY GAUDET

A BIG PART OF THE SHOBAC STORY is the legacy of the Ghost International Architectural Laboratory, better known as Ghost Lab or Ghost. Conceived by Brian and launched in 1994 as a summer course for his students at Dalhousie, Ghost grew into an internationally acclaimed annual workshop. In the architectural education field back then, it was one of the earliest voices in the design-build movement, so called, or what's more generally referred to as experiential learning: where students *learn by doing* within a hands-on, mentoring or training process that goes beyond sitting restlessly on their butts in a seminar room, as relevant as that form of instruction still is.

In its most mature state, Ghost attracted some thirty participants from around the world each year to Shobac—students, architects, engineers, builders, guest critics. For two intense weeks they worked together to design and build a mostly wood structure. The outcomes were often, it seems in retrospect, one half the product of group research into a compelling architectural question, and the other half a work of Land Art, a poetic if temporary landscape form. Imagine twin barns that look like dueling lanterns, a wind-testing tunnel, a land-surveying platform, a giant wing. The early projects were basically follies—experiments not meant to last. Some looked amputated from a schooner or barnyard, others were more abstract. All were open to the elements yet sheltering. Ghost lasted for nearly twenty years and produced a dozen experimental design-build projects, half of them now destroyed. The rest were built as permanent dwellings that still exist as major elements in the built environment at Shobac today.

The destroyed Ghost structures exert a strong hold on me, their absence a reminder of the power of memory, the cognitive residue of *what was* in shaping *what is*. Some days at Shobac I'm only capable of seeing what's no longer here. I find myself inside an alternate world to the moment at hand, equal in substance to the visible or present one. I see the missing structures among the existing ones and recall the stories of their making. I see how they relate to the buildings still standing, or born later, not just at Shobac but wherever Brian has built.

The ghosts that linger at Shobac are more than events in a histori-cal chronology of its settlement. They're ideas about architecture that have shaped Brian's practice for decades, and even now swirl around the valley with a message for those with an ear to listen.

Ghost 1, 1994

Nine students bivouacked in tents on a drumlin ridge. A makeshift john in the woods. Meals cooked on camp stoves. Beers around a bon-fire. A hole dug behind a log—the toilet. Debates about architecture under the stars. Lulled to sleep by the sonic caress of the breeze and the tides. And best of all, building something cool in a valley by the sea.

To some in the group the project sounds more like art than archi-tecture, something the landscape artist Christo would attempt. In this case, it's raising the gabled skeleton of an early Cape Cod house over an ancient stone foundation, built with a frame of white spruce from trees they'll harvest on the hill, then wrap the whole deal in fiberglass tarp and light it up from inside when all is said and done.

A ghostly presence in the landscape, that's the idea.

Why, one dubious student asks Brian around the fire pit.

After a pause, Brian says to the group. "Well, close your eyes and imagine a foggy midsummer's night. A night like tonight."

Some close their eyes, a few watchfully don't.

"Now imagine flying over the ghost of an abandoned village at the end of the world."

He lets that sit—what more really needs to be said?

That we're bringing a shrine to life? Conducting a shamanistic rit-ual to speak to those long gone but who linger here and deserve respect for what they've left behind? What point are we really making about the essence of things and of architecture in particular, that it's more about the spirit around and inside the outcomes of hammer and nail, what's invisible but real? That inspiration is equally related to memory, to what has come before, as it is to what will come, our dreams of the future?

Let them experience the making and the result.

Let the work speak for itself—

On the bell curve of commitment to the project, one young man stands out for his zeal: a gentle giant from Newfoundland,

108

Talbot Sweetapple who, in Brian's eyes, is as smart as they come yet totally unaffected, ready to dive into the project one thousand percent. When it comes time to cut down the trees to build the frame, he's the volunteer who climbs up the trunks, maybe thirty or forty feet in the air, and then rocks back and forth, coaxing the tree down to the ground where it can be stripped of limbs and bark. It's a dangerous process. The tree, with him riding it, could crash to the ground, thunderously, from a great height, severely injuring or killing him. He could be stabbed on the way down by the tree—or another tree in the area—with its *widowmakers,* the javelin-like limbs with arrow-sharp ends.

Talbot's rocking, his fearlessness, weirdly reminds Brian of a surreal scene from *Dr. Strangelove* when the American general, played by Slim Pickens, is seen astride a launched nuclear missile heading toward the Soviet Union, as if riding a bucking bronco.

Up Talbot goes time after time, rocking one tree after another, back and forth, over and over, until they have what they need.

One night over dinner, Brian asks the group, "How many of you believe you'll be able to make a living practicing architecture?"

Only one hand goes up: Talbot's.

All these years later, Talbot and Brian are partners in practice.

On the final night, a party. It just happens, like a sudden change in the weather, a natural or spontaneous occurrence.

Neighbors show up unannounced, some two hundred people, curious about the illuminated silhouette of a house, a strange beacon in the landscape, a giant lantern made of bonfire light that glows eerily orange through the tarp, a fiery apparition filtering into and through the heavy fog. Only four bottles of beer to go around but no one seems to care. There's music too, fiddles and squeezeboxes, voices.

Inside the tarp, in what today is called the SkyRoom, some folks are telling ghost stories for the fun of it. It's a habit Brian and Marilyn will pick up to entertain their young children.

Among the local visitors is a farmer who has pastured a herd of cattle in the field where the Ghost house was built.

All night long people come and go from the party, bumping up against large cows wandering in the dark.

Cowshit everywhere, on everyone's feet.

Ghost 2, 1995

On a fine sunny morning Norman Mossman stands bemused on the ridge while looking at Brian's students at work in the valley below. He's a local farmer in his fifties, in overalls, a man sturdy with muscles not from the gym. His cattle are pastured in the field where the students are working, which makes some uneasy about the bovine visitors. Will they attack? The cows munch hay and drop patties, indifferent to everyone.

Mossman is curious about what the students are doing. It doesn't look like work to him. But he's an open-minded man, an aspect of his character that has served him well as a community leader, a man capable of running the volunteer fire department and getting a resolution passed at the farm co-operative in town.

As he watches a group of young men attempting to drive wooden posts into the ground, some kitted out in baseball caps on backwards on their heads, some in open-toed sandals not proper work boots, he feels annoyance rising in him, a strain of psychological bile that he long ago learned only interferes with clear thinking and neighborly relations.

What in God's name are they building?

What are you up to this year, Brian?

He strolls casually down the hill, pausing at a respectful distance from the action so as not to be perceived as interfering.

Brian comes over to greet his neighbor, their relationship one of mutual respect, the older man always amenable to addressing the younger one's questions about farming and how the weather around here really works. They exchange pleasantries before Brian explains that the Ghost project this year will be a hundred-and-twenty-foot-long narrow platform, supported by two fabricated timber beams, spanning nine pairs of posts driven into the ground. It's basically a stage they're building, more or less. Its length extends from inside the old stone foundation over to an abandoned well that had been dug by the early settlers who were, as it happened, the farmer's distant ancestors.

Brian tells Mossman that constructing the platform, as simple as the job looks, is a real learning experience for his students. For some, it's the first time they've been on a building site. The goal is to build what Brian says is a land-surveying device to help his students better understand the qualities of this historic landscape, and where the ideal places are to build, given the weather and climate here.

Brian knows that once the platform is built—a long blade of a structure—some of his students will be shocked at how undulating the land below it is. The lesson here is that understanding topography is not a faculty native to many but rather a learned skill, an important one for an architect who intervenes in the landscape.

A land-surveying device, the farmer thinks.

Is that right?

Their conversation continues as they wander over to a student leaning on a sledgehammer, panting from his failed exertions in driving a post into the ground. He's hit the thing several times and each time the post bounces up and falls over dead, undriven, into the field.

The sledgehammer isn't a Home Depot special for the first-time DIY-er. It's an epic power instrument. The head is a massive block of black ebony, impaled on a solid steel bar. It's not something you lift never mind swing without calling your entire body into the discussion.

"Boy, you are working for the hammer," Mossman says, surprising himself and Brian by the hardness in his voice.

The student, who is triathlete-fit, and like many of his peers will possess at least two university degrees before entering the workplace a few years later, doesn't quite understand the farmer's words but catches the tone, which critical as it is, wasn't meant to insult.

Mossman looks around. The exhausted student is one of several young men either lying or stumbling around, exhausted, defeated by the sledgehammer. Mossman feels half-sorry for them, knowing as he does that driving posts into the dry summer ground is nearly impossible without a practiced snap of the wrists. It's like taking a snap shot with a hockey stick. It's a *knack*. It takes practice to do never mind perfect.

The farmer knows the kid is humbled and now only too willing to hand the epic sledgehammer over to him for a tutorial.

Every time the farmer hits that post, to the student's amazement, the much older man drives it in another four inches.

Ghost 3, 1997

> An elongated tubelike form twelve feet wide, eight feet high, and one hundred and twenty feet long was erected on undulating ground...The design of the 'wind tunnel," as it was called, imparted to architectural students an understanding of the wind forces and the effects they can have on an ultra-light timber structure...Ghost 3 was erected on an existing deck left over from the Ghost 2 project...the outer-wall skin was composed of alternating translucent and transparent panels of corrugated polycarbonate...Open bays allowed glimpses into the interior as well as views out to the surroundings.
>
> —AN ESSAY ON GHOST 3 BY KARL HABERMAN

They built a shrine to my presence, a vessel for their understanding. I honor their willingness to learn what they should have already known. I speak to the wisdom asleep inside them.

From the west I fly towards the valley over the waters of the estuary, the force of my intent speckling whitecaps here and there.

I am known by many names and speak in many voices.

In my gentler moods, in the warmth of summer, their faces turn thoughtlessly towards me, eyes closed, spirits risen.

In the colder months I draw blood to their cheeks.

I rage.

I ravage coastlines. I tear away their roofs and diminish the powers that light and warm their dwellings. I confront the vanity in their dreams of permanence in what they build.

I have known this valley and eaten at its cliffs long before human time. I have attacked the fields of those who first cleared the land, and my exuberance continues to sway the trees and ripple the ponds.

Their animals announce my presence before I arrive.

I cause their dwellings to lean and degrade in measurable time.

The taproot of their apple trees—the anchor of their resilience—grow towards me through the ground and keep their trunks upright against the indignities of my rhythms, a sign of respect from one elemental force towards another.

Their shrine touches the ground so lightly.

I will ultimately destroy it through no fault of their own.

Through the course of time, the connection between the posts and the deck rotted. One day a mighty storm finally brought about the collapse of the tube...Once again, nature undeniably had the upper hand over human endeavor.

—AN ESSAY ON GHOST 3 BY KARL HABERMAN

Ghost 4, 2002

Up on scaffolding near the roof, Bob Benz, a fullback of a man in his forties, crouches on one leg. The other leg is in the air, bent at the knee. Resting on his airborne thigh is a wet and very heavy 16-foot-long hemlock beam that teeters in the breeze. He appears effortless in driving four-inch spikes into the wood in single taps, one after another. This isn't heroic posturing for dramatic effect. It's what comes naturally to him, as if he were born in the air, hammer in hand, descended from a place in the sky where master builders come from.

On the ground, Brian stands with a group of students, young men who look up awestruck at his close friend and long-time collaborator hammering away above. What Brian knows, and none of the students do not—most not having a surplus of building experience—is that driving spikes into wet hemlock—a dense wood species—is a tricky chore on the ground, never mind up on a roof only half-constructed.

"You, you and you," Bob says gruffly at a pause, pointing at three students gawking up at him. "Up on the roof with me. Now."

The guys look back, speechless, all wondering: me? Us?

He doesn't have to say another word. The fullback presence isn't menacing but he means it. The students exchange uncertain glances. But soon they're all on the roof and doing just enough to help out and feel like they might actually like being asked to do more. Safety is the first and main thing on Bob's mind but with that priority well served, he's getting them to test the limits of what they're capable of. The students find the challenge both inspiring and humbling.

Bob and Brian's friendship goes back to graduate architectural school at UCLA. Bob grew up on a dairy farm in upstate New York, his father also a builder. Over the years Bob gravitated toward the craft disciplines of the profession, the skills and techniques of the building process. For nearly ten years, he worked with Brian on projects in Nova Scotia. He also married Brian's Acadian cousin, Rena, with Brian serving as best man. Brian thinks of their enduring friendship and trust in one another as the glue in the best kind of collaborative model, the merging of the sensibility and skills of the designer-architect, Brian, with those of the master builder, Bob. If there's one lesson Brian hopes the students take away this year it's the idea that collaborative intensity, the integration of the art and building crafts of architecture, is what in the end delivers the best outcomes. Not autocratic solo genius, which is what too many of his students are too happily willing to believe.

This year's project is the first Ghost workshop done outside the oversight of the university. From now on it will be run as a "small business" that will lose money every year but, regardless, will maintain its allure in connecting Brian to a growing network of international colleagues while providing a laboratory to explore ideas that will shape his practice. At times he jokes to his friends and peers that Ghost is basically a clubhouse for people like himself: boonie architects who somehow found their way into the profession in a meaningful way.

The project this year is to build over the ruins in the valley of two stone foundations, one each for the barns of two brothers, Simeon and Wilson, who lived here in the late 1700s. The space between the old foundations is about the width of a farm gate.

The result is a one-story wooden box over both ruins, latticed in layers of board, an opening in the middle suggesting the gateway. It's the charged space, between the two original barns. Brian wants his students to appreciate the sophistication of people from a time and place where there were no property lines or legally enforced modes of land inheritance. He wants them to understand how people settled and negotiated their world before the lawyers changed everything. He wants them to see that the democratic impulse to share, and share fairly, living side by side, was native or respected as a community-building force long before liberal democracy was formally invented.

One night, in the second week of the project, after a long day on the site, the famished team is seated around a long table, all slurping away at a delicious fish soup. This week, unlike the first, which was the design phase, everyone's doing real manual labor. Many are clearly eating twice the portions of the first week, which does not go unnoticed by one of the builders. "An army marches on its stomach," he says.

Bob Benz, who is sitting opposite Brian, pauses and holds up his spoon to the light, turning it around slowly to study it, amused, but silently so, being a man of few words.

"What's wrong, there?" Brian says.

Bob says nothing but there's a look—

"As it happens," Brian says, rising to the bait, anticipating what's to come. "The spoon is an Arne Jacobsen we bought at MOMA."

Bob keeps turning it around.

The spoon is a sleek device. To one art history major observing this exchange between friends, it seems inspired by Brancusi: sculpturally beautiful but perhaps deficient in soup-holding performance.

"I'll trade you a Jacobsen for a spoon," Bob says, deadpan.

Ghost 5, 2003

The completed project is a cross between a large tent and a wooden awning, 90-feet long, built over a frame of recycled telephone poles. The monopitched roof, wrapped in muslin, inclines up sharply toward the estuary from its 10-foot height at the lower end to the 30-foot apex, then angles down toward ground as a rectangular screen, as if an extension of the cliff below it. In elevation, the structure is an upside-down L-shape that looks like a giant wing or—when illuminated—a lantern. It's both stately and dynamic in its sculptural clarity and sheltering presence. Brian knows the design is original, as a wing-like form, but what he can't know is that it will become a signature element in several of his more celebrated buildings in the years ahead.

Tonight at the closing party, a crowd gathers under the structure, entranced by the Acadian folk singer Lennie Gallant with his guitar and band on a nearby stage while, outside, a bonfire roars into the darkness. A classic Nova Scotia summer night on the coast, chilly, foggy. Some are wrapped in blankets, others warmed by hot toddies, all in the grip of Gallant's songs of lament and perseverance that honor people on the rural and economic margins, the local heroes striving for dignity and searching for meaning in an unforgiving world.

Off to one side, there's an unlikely duo in conversation, both leaning against a column. It occurs to Brian that both men have, themselves turned into columns, virtually part of the new structure.

116

One figure is Kenneth Frampton, every inch the white-haired Columbia professor and world-class critic. He's the Ionic column, a slender and subtle presence. He's engaged in conversation with a younger, heavily bearded man who appears to be chiseled out of a granite boulder, Greg Ernst. He's the Doric column, a heavyweight presence.

Frampton's global reputation rests in part on his writings about "critical regionalism" that feature the work of architects—Brian among them—who reject the more banal forces of globalization and consumerism in favor of an architecture more sensitive to place, landscape, climate and culture—a new marriage of local tradition and global modernity. Frampton is one of the first guest critics at Ghost, and he's here this year to write an essay about the project.

Ernst is a famous strongman, finishing high up in World Strongman competitions years back, and twice the winner of the Canadian Strongman title. He once back-lifted two cars, complete with drivers at the wheel, weighing in total some 2,422 kilograms, a Guinness World Record. He has the distinction of having lifted more weight than any other human being in recorded history. Now he's a local dairy farmer and blacksmith from up the road, a neighbor here tonight with his wife and children just for the fun of it.

Brian is studying the Frampton-Ernst conversation covertly, unable to look away from moments like this that inspire him.

It's a time in many creative disciplines where critics are talking about the relationship—the tension—between the qualities of "high brow" and "low brow" in the forms and artifacts of cultural expression.

High-brow meaning: schooled in the history of ideas and creativity and alert to how a work fits within the context of its time and everything that came before and could come after. This is Frampton's world. High-brow suggests perspectives acquired and debated in seminar rooms and journals. Academic thinking, philosophical, conscious of what it is.

Low-brow meaning: coming out of everyday lives and from craftspeople who may not have advanced degrees or an excess of book learning, but have skills and perspectives, like Ernst does, developed out of the rituals and practical needs of their own culture and its tradition of making. It suggests creativity learned from mentors in the barnyard and the shipyard, the blacksmith shop and the building site. It privileges street smarts and rural savvy over classroom wisdom.

Action over words. People who do and make things you can see, touch, live in.

As Brian watches Frampton and Ernst gabbing away, both having a good time as a foot-stomping turn in the music takes the party up a notch, he sees in the moment two sides of a rare coin, a beguiling fusion of what's potentially native but not always reconciled in everybody who aspires to make or create anything.

It isn't the words high or low that speak to Brian. It's the unifying conjunction—the glue—between them: high *and* low.

Isn't unity, he wonders, the true if elusive marker of timeless quality? Isn't it proof there's only one world?

Ghost 6, 2004

There are enough advanced degrees and professors in the valley, Brian thinks, to staff a university faculty.

From the hilltop where he's standing on a windy day, he tries to make sense of a heated argument down below among a group of Ghost participants. Evidently, it's about how best to determine the horizontal level between the two towers they're building some two hundred feet apart. It appears the technique in favor is a string-level stretched between the two barn sites. There is, however, a faction in vocal rebellion, and continuing signs of animated outrage.

Coming up the hill towards him is Gordon MacLean, the master builder who has supported the Ghost program for years. In his early sixties, wiry strong, and long one of Brian's most trusted colleagues, he fits the stereotype of the martial arts master with the gentle presence to help the novices, the grasshoppers, learn the secrets of the trade.

"What do you see, Brian?" MacLean says softly.

Brian's not sure how to put it: there's a lot education and brain power in the field, for sure, but maybe not a ton of skill.

The string-level when seen against the pure blue straightness of the ocean horizon is sagging like it's some kind of skipping rope nearing the bottom of its cycle.

"I see the horizon, Gordon."

"That's God's level," he says, grinning.

5-E

MacLean is one of Brian's heroes, not just because of his mastery of a profession essential to the quality of his own work but because the man is an unofficial but tireless social worker, a genuine community leader. MacLean has long hired men out of prison—guys who have done real time, hard time. He puts them to work on his crews, trains and mentors them, gives them a sense of dignity and hope, staying true to the roots of his 60s counterculture optimism that you can make the world a better place one gesture and one person at a time. That optimism is schooled by a quiet diligence, a virtue respected in the Annapolis Valley farm community where he grew up and where, as a young man, he befriended the renowned painter Alex Colville, also a friend of Brian's, and himself someone who gives small-town values a good name.

Here at Ghost for another year, MacLean has left his wife and children behind in Dartmouth for two weeks and, again, steps into classic pied-piper mode, opening up his deep bag of builder tricks to the youngsters with an open mind. Like Brian, he's having less success this year with the professors who talk more than listen.

"You think it could get physical," he says to Brian referring to the folks arguing below but knowing it won't. It's play-fighting.

The project taking shape is a variation on the brief for Ghost 4 where the idea then was to interpret the ruins of foundations of two barns that were built side by side by the brothers Simeon and Wilson in the later 1700s. This time, the barns are less abstractions tied at the hip, but real buildings near the cliff face, speaking to each other across a field. The result will be two rectangular towers, framed using different techniques and subtle in their differences but alike enough in their DNA, like two brothers would be.

These brother-towers will be torn down years later, their guts recycled into other Ghost projects or cremated in bonfires. But on the night of the closing party, as Brian comes over the hill at sunset to oversee the preparations down by the stage, he's taken aback by the permanence they convey. It's like they've been there forever, upright sentinels, addressing the ocean, framing the space between them for the eye to contemplate the calm planes of the estuary as it shimmers in the fading minutes of sunset, now diffused through deepening fog.

Up on the rampart-styled roof of one tower, a lone bagpipe comes to life, the opening bars of a melancholic Celtic lament. Brian squints up where the internationally renowned bagpiper, Ian Mackinnon, is kicking off the festivities, using the power of song as an invitation to the hundreds of people now streaming down the road to the party.

For Brian, it's a surreal moment, a little uncontrollable, too, a local *Burning Man* experience. For years now, word of the Ghost closing parties has been spreading around the province, and tonight the crowd is almost too big to handle. As he'll later learn, cars have been backed up the road to Rose Bay. Maybe a thousand people will show up, causing some irritation among a few neighbors.

But right now, the party beginning, Brian is enjoying himself, lost in the music. It's a song composed in the 1700s in a Scottish prison by an infamous Robin Hood, Jamie MacPherson, as he awaited execution. The story is, he played the tune right up on the gallows, the rope around his neck, then leapt to his death before he was pushed.

Untie these bands from off my hands
And give me to my sword
There's not a man in Scotland
I won't brave at my word

* * *

In the 1990s Ghost was more than a rejection of the status quo in architectural education. It was what Brian calls a utopian gesture in presenting an alternative to the existing standard of practice. In Brian's words: "Ghost is rooted in the hands-on master-builder tradition, emphasizing an intimate interaction between master and apprentice in response to the increasingly virtual nature of architectural design."

Ghost rejected the ethos of the bureaucratizing university system as it expanded after World War Two and in the process privileged classroom academics over architectural practitioners with divided loyalties, having one foot in the commercial world, outside the campus. Brian believed that more training of architects should be done out in that world, in the field, on building sites, in communities where buildings are built, under the guidance of expert practitioners, not expert academics who may have built little or nothing at all. He believed architectural practices weren't doing better in mentoring architects, exploiting young graduates as cheap labor, hired or fired as the economy fluctuated. Many in his generation of architects felt the same, but he did something about it. As he told me, quoting Kenneth Frampton, "A school of architecture is likely not the best place to learn to be an architect.'"

For years Brian lectured at architecture schools around the world about Ghost, establishing his voice in the debates of the profession. After all, he was a tenured professor himself, so in addition to building his own practice, he felt that it wasn't enough to complain about how architects were trained. He had to practice what he preached.

"Ghost was about more than teaching people how to hold a hammer and wear a tool belt, all that macho stuff," he tells me. "It was much more about the social art of collaboration. On the best Ghost projects, there was equality in the moment, not the kind you find in the relativistic paradise of the university. Quality mattered. So a meritocracy took hold in those two weeks every year. The leaders led, the experienced coached the inexperienced, and everyone found their level of participation. The students were drawn to that. They weren't orphaned in a totally self-built sandbox without expert instruction where you discover just how creative you are, no, not that romantic bullshit."

Brian says Ghost was more than a resistance movement or guerilla warfare against the orthodoxy in architectural education. For him it was about nurturing the architect in himself by providing a formal boundary, or safe haven, from the compromises and distractions of our culture that still isn't supportive of principled architects. Here, in his valley, his sandbox, working with his students and colleagues, he could do whatever he wanted, and did. What he wanted his students to experience was an act of architectural transfiguration: how do you get people building a simple shed to believe they're building a cathedral?

Brian sees an analogy in Ghost to monasteries in the Middle Ages. "These were centres of learning in many fields, philosophy, science, agriculture, spirituality. They were outposts of optimism and innovation. And through their writing and learning the monks did change the world. So today, because of the media and the expanding global information culture, places like Ghost, even if very small in the grand scheme of things, can also be outposts of change, and have an impact by being fully local and yet international at the same time."

Ghost 7, 2005

Jet-lagged after the red-eye home from a trip to the opposite coast, Marilyn decides to forget about sleep this morning and stroll over from their farmhouse to see what's happening in the valley. As she nears the ridge above Shobac, in the breeze are the familiar sounds of a construction crew, the hammers, the buzz and whine of power tools, people shouting for this and that.

What soon comes into view are the skeletons of four new cabins, all lined up in the valley, facing the estuary. She wonders if it's all real, can't be, better not be, then marches down to the reality on the building site, where Brian separates himself from the group at work today.

"What's going on?" she asks, suddenly feeling fatigue that wasn't there ten minutes ago. "I thought we agreed you were just building a shed. *One* small building."

"Well, we need a place for the students to stay. If it's a campus."

Last summer she'd seen the first sketch of the four cabins that he did over lunch on a patio in Athens. But she'd didn't think he'd actually build them all at once, not given the costs involved.

"Brian, they're going to cost money to finish!"

"We can get a mortgage."

A long pause. "And how will we pay that mortgage?"

"We'll rent them out."

"We'll do what? If we're going into the rental business, Brian, it would have been nice to know in advance."

The expansion in the building program owed something to a student enrolled this year at Ghost, a young Chinese-Canadian woman. She said, hey, let's build something real this year. Like permanent architecture!

Brian took the bait, deciding to finally go all-in to pursue a dream that had been curdling in him for years: build a proper school here, an *institution*. And that means making places for people to work and experiment, but also a dormitory, a dining hall, a library. He can see it now: the four cabins creating a line across the valley...and, next year, he'll add another structure, or multiple structures, in a line adjacent and perpendicular to it. And with the cliff creating another line, he's got three sides of the rectangle of a courtyard, a *quadrangle*.

It all makes sense to him—

128

Less so to family finances.

This isn't the first time and it won't be the last that Brian takes the family towards debt-driven discomfort. But all that doesn't matter now. There's a vision activated. Come what may.

Ghost 8, 2006

Months before he does the first sketch, he sees the table floating on its own, a specific table for a specific place but also a table for all time and all places, as long and strong as a grown-up oak. He sees a hundred hands hovering over it, the communion of fifty voices in happy cross-talk, the percussive effects of cutlery on ceramic, the aroma and remains of a great meal, the candle wax and red wine stains after a party that went a little too late.

The building in which this table will live is the Studio and it will stand on a foundation of transverse concrete fins, its monopitched roofline rising steeply toward the estuary. The Studio will join the four cabins in consolidating two sides of the quadrangle, or courtyard, the heart of a valley campus. Designed as a dining hall and meeting space for Ghost participants, the Studio arises as an exercise in experience and improvisation in about two weeks. The first phase is design, led by Brian, then construction led by Bob Benz and Gordon Maclean.

Ghost 8 is a folk-tech process at high speed, no cranes or heavy machinery, just scaffolding as the need arises, block and tackling, and people carrying lumber around for maybe the first time in their lives. The roof trusses, the guts of the structure, are built and installed in one day from a truckload of angle iron, cut down in size with a mini grinder operated by two students from Mexico City. The idea was to size the iron pieces so that the four women assigned to the job could lift them over their heads for welding in place by Big Al, a local welder who has long been part of the builder scene locally. The concrete fins, serving as the foundation, were poured in a single morning by Brian and two architects, David Miller and Bob Benz. They worked together in a leisurely flow like a team of cooks prepping meals in time for lunch.

As the project nears completion, the building shell complete, another mortgage is required for interior work to continue.

Brian wonders whether the Studio would have been better designed had there been months to do it, and right now he doesn't believe so. He's pleased with the water-facing bay window that wraps around a corner of the building. He tells someone that when it comes time for him to die, he wants to be taken by a big wave coming through that window, an echo of a comment made to him years ago by a mentor, Charles Moore.

In recent years the project-ending Ghost community parties have been getting rowdier with people crashing in from all over the county and beyond. This year, a cohort of what can only be called belligerent assholes join the crowd: young men from town who are drunk or stoned or both, according to a village elder on hand that night. Some have had trouble with the law before as it later turns out.

When Marilyn intervenes in the later stages of the party to ask the troublemakers to leave, she gets thrown to the ground by one of them. The man who does that, then takes a swing at Brian and Marilyn's daughter, Ali, only to have Bob Benz's mitt come out of nowhere, clamp down on the swinging arm before the blow lands and, in one motion akin to an Olympic shot-putting motion, throws the offender into the air...who lands with a crash on a scrap lumber pile.

130

The racket stuns everyone.

Seconds later, Benz's knee is anchored to the man's neck. It takes several people to pull him away.

The guy still hasn't had enough.

"Come on, old man, let's get it on," he shouts after getting up.

"No, we won't get it on," Benz says slowly, "Because you don't know who you're dealing with. Because I will actually kill you."

Someone intervenes to prevent the killing, but the guy is still not through and now seeks to take on Gordon MacLean.

"Violence, is that it?" MacLean says, heating up. "I'll show you violence. But it'll be the last thing in this world you'll ever see."

Violence is wisely averted and, soon enough, the troublemakers retreat from the party, although later that night, much later, the RCMP arrest one of them for more foolish behavior in the village.

In the days following a number of local men who had left the party before the melee get in touch with Brian to apologize for not being around to help out and to defuse matters. Brian senses their embarrassment at how some young folks are turning out, although it's no mystery to anyone. The troublemakers are part of a story that still plays out today in rural communities where the death of agrarian economies hasn't been followed by something sustainably new for too many men seeking but not finding a dignified way of life, if you discount the minimum wage tourism jobs or working as security guards at one of the big-box stores in town.

"Still not right, no matter the cause, no excuse," one man, a retired lobster fisherman, gloomily tells him one morning while they're sitting around the Studio having coffee. "In the old days, we would have tossed them on the roof of a truck, drove to the beach, and then beat the living daylights out of them—unless their parents did it first."

Brian nods in all the right places, not making too much of it, but he's really been shaken. And later wonders why. No one really got hurt, disaster was avoided, the good guys won, the mob turned back. So why so upset? He's seen much worse in his life. It will take some time to process the events but he'll wake up one day realizing that, in this instance, what had been violated was his idealism—his utopian perspective—about Ghost as an enterprise in community-building.

Sometimes you can do all the right things with the best intentions, he thinks, and still things can go very wrong: the fall from grace—the loss of faith—so much harder the more idealistic the dream.

Ghost 9, 2007

It's a test, a variation on the question: if you lead horses to water, will they drink?

Will Ali's two horses willingly enter the new barn—technically, a loafing barn—built for them, the outcome of the Ghost project just completed? If they refuse to enter, or do so only after excessive coaxing, this will represent for Brian, who's watching the scene unfold from up on the ridge, a pyrrhic victory of form over function.

Conditions couldn't be better. It's a sweltering August day at high noon, windless. The horses have had enough of the sun and heat by now.

As Ali leads the horses towards the barn from across the field, Brian tells himself that the horses won't be persuaded by any back story or design brief about how the barn came to be. They'll either like it or not. Initially, there's a tentative response, a definite pause in forward motion, the horses being instinctually suspicious of the many strategies deployed by their human companions to house, exercise and care for them. But their trust in Ali trumps the moment as she encourages them onwards in soothing tones and familiar blandishments.

And soon enough they amble into the open bays inside the lean-to and there they hang around, munching oats, drinking, resting. Happy.

Mission accomplished.

As Shobac starts to look like a campus, it does so without compromising its purpose as a small farm. Which makes total sense to Brian. In his reading of cultural history, there's a long but inevitable line of architectural evolution that leads from the farm barnyard to the monastic cloister to the campus quadrangle and, finally, to the town square. From the reality of settlement and the agriculture required to support it, you grow into more sophisticated institutions. You get architecture. You get education. You get horses in loafing barns.

The priority of the moment is this: every farm needs a loafing barn for the animals to hang out in and take shelter from the elements. This barn, situated behind the campus quadrangle created in the previous two Ghost projects, creates a second courtyard or barnyard in the valley in the north-east corner. Two courtyards, or barnyards, is the norm in county farms. Near the barn, one outdoor space is for the manure and wood piles, the grittier back office, while the front courtyard near the cabins, south-west facing, is where pretty flowers are grown and you can stroll around, shooting the breeze at the end of a long day.

While farming functionality provides the practical inspiration here, the barn is also radically sculptural. It channels design elements that conspire to create a unique expression in local farm-building vernacular. It's mainly a lean-to shed, an archetypal form known in many agricultural cultures, open at the front for animals to enter and exit, with a sheltering roof over them. That's its job. But the structure is also a modernist wedge with a slanting, monopitched roof. The building isn't so much anchored to the ground but hangs there, elevated a few feet above, a cantilever held up by two lines of telegraph poles and trusses that act like dividers between the six bays. It's a dynamic composition, a long rectangle that appears to be rotating over itself toward you while the roof tilts upwards along its length.

A few days after the Ghost party, Brian walks down into the valley one evening for a moment alone. He needs a good look again.

After plugging in flood lights in the barn, he walks away a distance through the field before turning back. And when he does, the barn announces itself as a lantern, as he knew it would, echoing the first Ghost, the tarp-draped Cape illuminated in the fog.

This loafing barn is also a lying down version of one of the towers built during Ghost 6, the one called Simeon. That tower was archetypal in the sense of being a building you'd likely find on the archeologically rich coastlines of Turkey or Scotland, or in farm country of the American Midwest or a Swiss canton. That Ghost 6 tower could be found anywhere in the global inventory of agricultural communities.

This tower is, in Brian's mind, the "female" version of Simeon, which he christens Beulah, in honor of the memory of Beulah Oxner, his neighbor, the village matriarch who with husband Albert welcomed Brian and Marilyn into the community years ago now.

Female? How so, one student asked.

The barn would need to be place-specific and fully sensitive to the landscape around it, like the woman herself. The barn had to be more than archetypal, more than a timeless form in the vocabulary of human settlement. To be a fitting tribute to Beulah it really also had to be something that could only exist here, uniquely.

It doesn't look anything like a barn now—

It's more like a doorway, he thinks: a transportation device.

In the stillness of the moment, the illuminated barn emptied of the horses for the day feels otherworldly to him, a vehicle that seems capable of flying up and away into the mysteries of the night.

Ghost 10, 2008

"It's out of plumb," Gordon Maclean says, eyeing the half-built cabin on the ridge.

Brian can barely hear him over the generator but agrees.

The structure isn't much out of vertical plumb to be a visual or spatial irritation most would notice. Evidently not the students in the group, most of them milling around, wondering what the fuss is.

The young men, the gender majority this year, have become increasingly unfocused as the heat intensifies this morning. Most have stripped down to the waist. A few class clowns have manifested, evidently punch-drunk jokey after only a week of physical labor.

Brian and Gordon move off to the side to assess the problem and debate solutions. One young man, listening in, gets the idea that with all the muscle and testosterone among the guys here, they should be able to easily tilt the structure a couple of inches back to vertical straightness. There's a brazen effort to push the building straight that Brian and Gordon allow to proceed, knowing the outcome.

Half a dozen guys lean into the task—and fail.

Of course it's impossible to push a building straight by hand.

At this point in the project Brian feels like a long-suffering Dad, overwhelmed by the persistent corralling required of so much youthful student energy and, all too frequently, their disregard for basic construction site safety. The project has been something of a slog this year. Something hasn't fully jelled yet in the group.

In concept, the project is solid: build two boxes—or two parts of a house—on a ridge above the valley, connected by a thousand-foot courtyard. The box higher up will be a day pavilion, now shrouded in fog, a much cooler microclimate. It will provide a prospect to the sea beyond the landscape below. The lower unit will be a night pavilion, for sleep, for refuge, where all the heat and sunshine is right now.

"There's an old trick," Gordon shouts to Brian, who snaps off the generator. And that gets everyone's attention, the equivalent of a high school teacher slapping shut a textbook, serving notice to the mob.

Now Gordon asks a slender young woman to walk over to a pile of unseasoned lumber just arrived from the mill. He also asks her to find the floppiest, greenest length of 1x4 lumber she can find. What she comes back with looks like a spinach pasta noodle in Brian's eyes. Gordon nails one end to the parapet and the other to the floor, the wood sagging flexibly in the middle, like a bow string at rest. Next, he instructs the young woman to pull the floppy wood taut, towards her, using only one hand, as if arming the bow. And once she does that, no muscle required, the entire structure audibly shifts, not exactly a Frankenstein coming to life, but internal forces are being adjusted.

The structure is suddenly plumb. Straight as an arrow

Gordon quickly marshals a group to nail in diagonal braces to consolidate the victory against vertical crookedness.

Everyone else stands back in silent, bewildered admiration.

134

Ghost 11, 2009

Twelve feet in the air, two men stand close together on an old timber beam in the frame of the nineteenth-century Troop Barn. The building had been rescued from demolition in Annapolis Valley and brought to Shobac in parts. The men are guiding a column down through a slot in the middle of their beam to create a structural joint—

Their beam snaps in two—

Suddenly in the air, Brian and his friend, the architect Francis Keré, are surfing the falling beam, their gazes locked, both thinking—

Who are we going to kill beneath us?

Will we die here, together?

They're one man right now, one shared perspective in one scary moment moving so fast but experienced in timeless slow motion.

Down they go.

Images unfurl in a calming cadence through Brian's brain:

He sees their first meeting at a conference in Norway and the complicated handshake Francis teaches him, the way his hands stay on you longer than you initially think necessary, saying, where I come from, all we have is touch.

He sees the morning in Halifax when Francis, their house guest, comes into the kitchen in his white robes and asks Marilyn, would you like me to fetch your water for the day? He tells her that fetching water was his job in the family as a boy growing up in Burkina Faso.

He sees Francis gently picking up a picture of Brian and his father, saying, how beautiful, as I have no pictures of my father.

Down they go—and there's still endless time for Brian to think—

What he knows is that in this ride down to possibly serious injury or worse, Francis understands everything, how and why they met, what they're doing here, and what ultimately connects them.

A prince of a man, Brian thinks. Literally. An African prince, royalty in Burkina Faso, with the ritualized facial scars to prove it.

Africa's Louis Kahn, he thinks.

A mystic. A shaman.

Brian feels like he's looking into himself, at himself.

There's something in the layered reactions of the moment that will tell Brian what it means to be an architect: no matter where you're from, how you've been raised, or raised yourself, there are universal qualities we can aspire to in our work that cross cultures, eras, geographies.

So much unifies us if only we open ourselves to what the world really wants and needs from us.

If they die here, he realizes, they'll die in a building devoted to celebrating community, a space built for weddings, parties, random moments of public togetherness. Would they hold his funeral here?

His daughter had a dream that the Troop Barn should be sited at the lowest point in the land, up against the marsh that bleeds into the tidal lake. The idea being, the barn is so tall, we don't want it to dominate, but serve as one side of a new town square.

So down they keep falling—
Until they land on the floor, causing a violent boom—
And step off the broken beam together—
Unhurt—
A lifetime later.

Ghost 12, 2010

In the kayak he paddles my rippling surface as I rise and surge towards the sand. I work to the rhythm of the moon, the power of the cosmos. Again I fill the lake around this little cove as I've done and will do forever. This is a serene moment in my infinite pattern.

I am the soul of the sea. The tide.

The land he approaches on my surface is fragile, a tiny spit vulnerable to my coming-and-goings.

Here is where they once built shelters on the edge of possibility, on the boundary between land and the vast forces within me.

Here is where in summer they harvested shellfish in my absence and speared fish within me.

Everything human here from before has disappeared.

Yet here is where he has chosen to build again, the home for his kayaks, the first gesture in the return of what has been lost.

Will those he now brings here hunt within my depths again?

Or will they simply observe the mutable splendor of my moods?

He is tired from paddling over the endlessness of my skin, fearing the large fin of a Great White cutting through me towards him. He tells himself if it happens, he's had a good life, that his time has come.

So many forces live within me.

New forces now change my shape and darken the intensity in how I touch what is not me. Sooner or later I will destroy or bury everything within the waves of my eternal fortitude.

The house for his kayaks will endure—for how long?

It sits on two grey-white fins of hardened substance made from the essence of earthly power—rock, sand, clay, shale. From water too, my essence. These fins in the land allow me to explore and churn under the house, surrounding it in my extreme moments.

The fins do not block my passage but channel it.

I am indifferently tolerant.

For now.

* * *

Like most North Americans, I was raised an architectural illiterate. It's a condition I've worked to overcome with mixed results. Like any second or third language learned later in life, with architecture I struggle to keep up with the conversation at times, fairly often missing the precise or idiomatic turn of phrase available to those more fluent with the grammar and more experienced with the toolbox.

Architectural illiteracy is a topic hard to talk about without bruising egos. Like politics, religion and, increasingly these days, health care and nutrition, everyone's an expert on what a house should look and feel like, and what it says to the community and world around it. So many people I know often say, look, I know what I like.

The logic is, if I can buy or live in a house with my money (or the bank's), I must be an expert on what it is or should be.

The idea that in-depth learning about design and building practices might be a good thing doesn't occur to nearly enough people, judging by the quality of the architecture in North America built, say, in the past hundred years. I won't be the first or the last to say that most buildings and intentional communities that get built today are aesthetic and ecological mediocrities, arguably evidence of some combination of mass consensual ignorance, commercial rapacity and zoning stupidity. Other cultures—the Japanese and the Scandinavians come to mind—have done a better job (not always) of generally infusing the cultural situation with an expectation that people should at least understand their design and building traditions, that there should be some literacy in this area, some shared values about what constitutes a good building.

As a youngster, like many boys, I often had a hammer in hand and a tin of nails beside me. I crucified wood with verve and built little houses that instantly collapsed, boats that didn't float, and planes that didn't fly. There was no formal learning shared with me at any time about what a house was and how it should be built and why. No basic instruction in how communities actually got built and, in turn, shaped the quality of our lives and our social and commercial relations.

My father, who left school in grade four, owned a small machine shop, a magician at sculpting steel. I became conversant through him on how to operate a lathe, a milling machine, an arc welder. He taught me that steel could be as labile and warmly textured as wood. But in all my formative years in the school system there was no mandatory instruction in the history or the best practices of the built environment. We were inflicted with history courses across the humanities and social sciences. Yet not a peep about the history of building, the subject that literally puts a roof over our heads. In my day there were high school courses in carpentry, plumbing and draftsmanship but it was understood they were intended for indifferent or troublesome students who were not going on to university but to blue-collar jobs. The message was: being a carpenter or builder was a low-status career.

It's not worth looking back too strenuously at the limitations in one's education. But something so fundamental as housing, our built environment generally, strikes me as a topic where literacy should be expected of every citizen for the greater good.

If there were more emphasis on architectural literacy in our educational system, would things be any different?

This much is true: unless someone decides to study architecture or urban design or engineering after high school, we lack a compulsory rite of educational passage in this area of community well-being.

Architecture schools are for those with a declared interest, the field not acknowledged never mind respected as essential learning for every citizen. A shame—and a lost opportunity.

138

Ghost 13, 2011

After a month in Mali, camping out in the heat of the Sahara and paddling long days in canoes on the Niger winding through it, the journey of a lifetime into the oldest history of *settlement*, the birthplace of architecture, Brian finds himself alone in a sweltering waiting room of a busy airport, on his way home, exhilarated but sunburnt exhausted. What a trip! A chance to reconnect with valued colleagues who took the journey with him, all highly regarded architects, Rick Joy, Marlon Blackwell, Tom Kundig, Wendell Burnett, Peter Rich. His peers.

When the call comes through, the voice on the other end is tired but forceful. "I'm coming. I need to be with my friends."

Brian left for the trip only days after speaking to the Australian architect Glenn Murcutt, a good friend and long-time mentor, who had just lost a son to cancer. The last thing Brian expects is Glenn showing at the Ghost 13 symposium next week. And now he'll be there.

Days later at Shobac, the symposium preparations are just about complete, a labor of love (and stress) for Brian and his office. They're bringing in and caring for the needs of some two hundred visitors who include architects, critics and historians from a half dozen countries. A good number of them have serious reputations in the field either for their built work or their contributions to the critical discourse.

On the eve of the opening session, another call comes in on Brian's phone from the Toronto airport. The architect Francis Kéré tells him he's returning home to Burkina Faso and won't fly on to Nova Scotia to attend the symposium. His father, a tribal king, has suddenly died. Kéré, a prince who will become the new king of the tribe, arrives home too late to join the sixty thousand mourners at his father's funeral.

A son going home to grieve his father, Brian thinks. And a father, Glenn, coming here in grief over the death of a son.

He sees an omen in that symmetry of loss and pain. Already, this year's Ghost feels different, freighted with unanticipated meanings.

This Ghost is different in other ways. There's no building project this year. In part this is because Brian isn't sure what next to build and, anyway, he intends from now on to be less financially reckless in what he does here. He's taken the family finances to the limit too often at Shobac. Bottom line, he's unsure whether he wants Ghost to continue beyond this event. The financial hit, year after year, can't be ignored, along with the time taken away from his practice. He's also been stung by rumors that suggest he's taking advantage of unpaid student labor to improve the real estate value of the MacKay-Lyons properties. He disagrees, having lost money every year just to keep the program alive. Moreover, the student work is only a small part of the total costs in the buildings finished. But he finally admits to himself, no one cares about his logic or his accounting. What some people see are students working for nothing, not their passion to build something real.

All these doubts and concerns aside, he's not ready to give up on Ghost just yet, wondering if the symposium itself might suggest a new direction, or at least an affirmation that it makes sense to keep going.

As the presentations unfold one after another under the dome of the Troop Barn, Brian is resolved to stay mainly on the sidelines and be a facilitator, a host. There are plenty of insightful voices on hand to speak to the concerns shared by all about the sorry state of architectural education, a key theme here, and a subject on which Brian has tilted at windmills since the beginning of his career.

In the animated audience discussions that follow each speaker, the concerns expressed are similar to those shared by other professions trying to cope with a globalized, technology-crazed world. How the schools aren't doing a good job of training the next generation. How the newer digital means of production are problematic in tethering architects to simulated experiences on screens that flatten the world and degrade spatial awareness. There's handwringing over the effects of global capital and the corporatizing of architecture as an enabling handmaiden to profitability, but not always to nurturing best practices in design, never mind fealty to the timeless priority of building sustainable communities that elevate, not denigrate, the human experience.

It's a preaching-to-the-choir event in some respects. Where Brian senses the event moving into new territory has little to do with the formal intellectual concerns and ideological flashpoints. It's the moment when three men start a conversation on the porch of the Studio, a trio of respected elders, now in their middle to upper seventies: the Australian Glenn Murcutt, a Pritzker Prize winner, the Finnish professor-architect and writer, Juhani Pallasmaa, the celebrated poet of the profession, and the British critic, Kenneth Frampton, the Columbia professor.

These men, their work an inspiration to countless architects, are making small talk in the cold wet weather with the fog blowing in from

over the water. It occurs to others too that this is a special moment, and so a perimeter of separation now buffers them, everyone standing back. What's special for Brian has little to do with a celebrity moment. There's mortality in the air. These men aren't fragile, but they are visibly elderly. Their transition from robust middle age seems to have happened overnight, Brian thinks. Where have twenty years gone? What about the next twenty years which will also arrive overnight?

On the last day of the event Brian dials in Francis Keré from Burkina Faso on his cellphone, putting him on the speakerphone to deliver a presentation up on the screen in the Troop Barn.

Keré is apologetic about not being there because of his father's recent death, and in the thick silence that follows, Brian says, "I have someone who wants to talk to you."

He hands the phone to Glenn Murcutt—

So the father who lost a son, and the son who lost a father, exchange condolences, a physical world apart, but suddenly connected, and many in the barn feel connected too, caught up in the shifting emotional tide in the room and what happens at times, weirdly, when sadness shared with a crowd somehow lifts everyone's spirits.

Brian will later wonder why he turned the moment from the professional to the personal. It's just not something you automatically do at a symposium. There's always the risk of compromising the situation. Do people really want their emotions yanked around during a PowerPoint session? Why not? After all, what's really holding this group together? The passion for the work, yes, but of course it's something much deeper: being friends in common cause over so many years of toil and struggle. In any case it just felt right to Brian. Like the tears streaming down his face and every other face in the room.

The morning after the symposium, each with long walking sticks, Brian and Pallasmaa stroll the hills around Shobac in the fog. Pallasmaa is a gentle presence, the philosopher-king you find in folk tales, silver hair to the shoulders, the silver beard, the scarf, the book nestled under one arm, the Finnish-accented English that sounds more formal than he really is.

The conversation is unhurried, with long gaps. "Brian, you know what is so special about this place and what you've done these many years, if I may be so direct," Pallasmaa says, pausing for Brian to respond, courteous to a fault.

"Juhani, continue, please, it's a privilege."

"It relates to something Merleau-Ponty said, if you will forgive my resorting to French phenomenology so early in the day. 'We come not to see the work of art, but the world according to the work.' I see so much of you here, what you cherish, but what I admire more is the unity of everything, how it reveals and celebrates the landscape and the community around it and its history. The object of art is ultimately the world—would you not agree?—not the inner life of the artist as interesting as that life might be, if you understand me."

It's a compliment that asks for silent acceptance, then Pallasmaa continues: "These buildings reveal and empathize essential features of the landscape and place. In a way the focus is less on them but outwards to the forests, meadows, fields, ocean bays, horizon, the skies. They really do turn into vehicles of the imagination."

This too gives Brian pause—

"Juhani, I've been meaning to ask you. Do you think I should keep this program going? Ghost. I'm just not sure."

It's Pallassma's turn to think things over—

As they keep walking, the fog thickens up. To Brian's eyes the silver mane of his friend keeps disappearing and then reappearing in the enveloping greyness, as if the man is performing a magic trick to highlight the creative forces floating within him.

"The most valuable part of the experience here is the most expensive," Pallasmaa finally says. "The hospitality of your family. It is such a precious resource, so easily wasted."

"That's true."

"It's time to let someone else have a go at this."

Brian lets that sink in—

Pallasmaa sees the questions on Brian's face. "Take some time," he says. "Time to reflect on what's next. And have that conversation with yourself I know you want and need to have.

6
Invisible Conversations with Brian MacKay-Lyons

SKYROOM LARRY GAUDET

The Practitioner: Frank Lloyd Wright

I'M TRUDGING ALONG IN THE ARIZONA DESERT like I've just stepped onto a moving walkway that isn't moving. It's the expectation of gliding—then disappointment when you're not. I'm battling resistance in each step, the limitations of myself in time and space. It's furnace-hot, a world without shadow at high noon. The breeze burns into me.

The desert, when contemplated from an abstract distance, much like the ocean and the prairie, can fool you into thinking it can be experienced with ease. How easy to underestimate nature.

On this dirt road flanking the front of Taliesen West, I'm watched in silence by towering saguaro cactuses all around me. From my vantage point, the visible planes of Wright's compound, the sloping geometries of its timbered structure and cantilevered rooflines, the layering of plinth forms, suggest a ruin from a lost civilization that knew things we still don't.

I step over the carcass of a small rodent, headless, shredded by who knows what.

He waits at the top of the pyramidal staircase behind the triangular reflecting pool, standing next to a petroglyph-etched boulder on its plinth. He's wearing a dark blue suit and matching cape over it. A darker blue silk scarf folds crisply inside his suit lapels, high and tight on his neck. The black broad-brimmed hat. The cane. He's not dressed for the desert, but in spite of it, the classic operatic Wright persona, our all-seeing Zeus, the thundering sky god of the architectural profession.

I figure he's not been exerting much psychic energy tracking my arrival. The closer I get, the more he appears to be looking past me, contemplating the brown vastness of the landscape below the thin blue of the Arizona sky. Suddenly he becomes real, a living presence: a man in his middle seventies now, fighting fragility, not a statue to my fantasies of who he might or should be.

As I climb the final step, his head dip towards me, the tiniest acknowledgement. He's looking at me directly now. It's not a negatively aristocratic gaze that judges everything before or below it. Although there is a feral inquisitiveness in play. I detect genuine curiosity about me. I also see the vulnerability in his eyes that strike me as an honest portal into the complications and conflicts of the man.

His handshake is soft, indifferent. Some part of him must demand remove from the supplicants on his doorstep. I respect the distance he creates. He's an elder to me and to architecture.

Wright's self-invention over decades into a larger-than-life character, grandiose, spendthrift, distinctly American, is the stuff of legend and headline-making scandal and personal tragedy. I wonder about the difference between the legend and the man. The evidence on balance is that he woke up one day not knowing the difference.

He gestures with his cane at the boulder with the petroglyph drawings. It features stick figures of humans and animals surrounded by geometric symbols that meant something to the Hohokam and Oasisamerican societies who lived around here in epochs long gone. The images are beautiful in their simplicity. From the distance across so much time, you still have a sense of the hands and hearts that transfigured imagination or shamanistic insight on rock.

"Perhaps we would have been advised to leave these boulders where they originally were," he says, his Midwestern drawl affected with a self-deprecating edge. Then, after clearing his throat, "You realize, the entire Southwest is a graveyard, a landscape ruin of bones and shell—of so many forgotten cultures."

I know something about building around a ruin at Shobac, and I'm about to say as much, but he's turned away to lead me inside. I'm soon enveloped in Wright's design grammar that, inside, features thick low-rise walls produced from an unusual structural concoction, a cheap local mix of rocks and concrete, poured inside forms lined with old carpets. In the main drafting room, each skylight bay is covered in canvas scrims to soften the harsh desert light. In silence, we wander through a labyrinth of pavilions, gardens, courtyards and pathways. Like Wright's best work, the compound relies on an open plan to break down boundaries between the indoors and outdoors, creatively introducing natural light into interior space, all the while making good use of local building materials. This place provides the complete Wright support system, his castle in the desert where he pursues his oversized dreams, the winter camp for himself, his family, his acolytes.

Soon we're outside again on a walkway under a lengthy pergola, ambling along through the striped shadows created by the crossbeams above us. He's in no hurry to direct the conversation. After all it's my psychological nickel we're spending here. Not sure where to begin, I jump in head first: "In a thousand years, I'd like to think the archeologists of the future will come along and discover this place as a temple ruin, much like Stephens did with the Mayans in the jungle. And they will astonish whatever our civilization has become by then."

He grimace-smiles, looking straight ahead. He's used to fulsome praise and while not impressed, he's not offended. I did the expected before the master. He stops and looks at me again.

"So what precisely are we here for, Mr. MacKay-Lyons?"

"Mr. Wright, I've tried over many years to model my practice on yours. I'm at another decision point, about where to go from here."

"Decisions come and go, don't they, that put our knickers into an existential uproar all too often," he cackles at me.

"Couldn't agree more, Mr. Wright."

It's Mr. Wright. Not Frank. I learned that from one of my mentors, Bruce Goff, my thesis advisor on my first professional degree.

Bruce had been a trusted associate of Wright's for years and always called him Mr. Wright, never Frank. That was the expectation. I learned so much from Bruce, a gentle Texan, listening to his stories of working beside Wright, much like I sat at the foot of my grandfather's rocking chair as a young boy, engrossed in his tales of life on the sea.

I'd be nowhere as an architect or a man without the mentors who saw something in me as I saw something in them.

"There are similarities between us, Brian, at least on the surface," Wright says. "We're country boys who acquired the patina of metropolitan sophistication, and then went home, to settle, protect the creative impulse, honor the agrarian tradition. Raise chickens, plough fields, live the rural idyll. And lick a few wounds, in my case. In yours?"

Hitting me with both barrels.

"I've been presumptuous," he continues, a gently mocking apology, now scrutinizing me more closely: "I'm sure we understand each other, Brian. Just because a man takes to wearing bespoke suits and collecting Japanese prints doesn't mean he's forgotten how to appreciate the smell of cowshit in the field after a summer rain."

He's teasing me with caustic precision. Does it open a door for me to do the same? No. Rhetorical jousting on equal terms isn't the way forward here. I need to be careful. It's wise to be wary of contrary signals to conscious intention that rise up from the depths and assert themselves. I really just want—need—to listen my way forward here.

"Mr. Wright, there are larger questions that you are uniquely qualified to answer, in my humble opinion."

The gaze gets more intense, and I feel the heat of it.

"You're not here looking for *permission*?"

Almost sarcastic now, as if welcoming me into what to expect in the arena of his mind, its hurricane forcefulness.

I just keep looking at him—

"Well, I'm glad," he concedes. "You don't seem the type. In my experience when a man of your ambitions arrives on my doorstep, I tend to think he's not looking for any answers he doesn't already have, somewhere inside, if perhaps not available to him always as needed. You're looking for fraternity of a kind. To enter a pantheon, from the back door or front, it doesn't matter. Something akin to that. Am I right?"

Possibly a compliment. My eyes remain locked into his.

"Your mother knew before you were born that you would be an architect," I say, repeating one of the famous anecdotes in Wright lore. "I knew at four. Knew I wanted to be you before I knew who you were."

"It's enticing to invoke destiny and the Fates with a capital F in our choices," he says, wearily, tapping his cane on concrete slab. "But it's a slippery slope. Because if you go too far in that belief, you'll find yourself believing the Creator Himself sent down an angel to invest you and you alone with the power to change the world."

"Isn't that what drives you?"

"I admit to the arrogance of that position. Early in life I had to choose between honest arrogance and hypocritical humility. An easy choice, I would think."

He laughs in a grumbling way.

He's like the desert itself here, a dizzying force, a limitless presence, despite his diminutive physical stature.

"Brian, let's clear the obvious questions from the drafting table."

I nod.

"You've come here because you are trying to unify the threads of your life in that valley by the sea. You're raising a family there. You are trying to do world-beating work. Writing books. Reaching your students to bring your ideas, not theirs, to refinement. You are a developer. And unintentionally I gather, in the tourism business. An entrepreneur."

"The unity of all things, that's part of it."

"But there's more. Shobac has become more than experiments now. You want buildings there that last. And you tell yourself that others demanded this of you. Take it from me, you want it for yourself."

"I don't—"

But he's not listening now—

"And now, here you are, the village architect you have so earnestly sought to be. The country doctor of your profession. Locally. One house call after another. Am I right?"

"There's an ideal in that."

"Although, be advised, a doctor can bury his mistakes whereas an architect can only advise his clients to plant vines."

We both chuckle, mirthlessly, into a silence I'm expected to fill but he gets there before I do. "The model for any practice is one thing, but the underlying purpose, are you clear on it? Seems your dreams go far beyond any village these days."

"My purpose hasn't changed at all."

"I would be honored if you'd enlighten me, then."

"Mr. Wright, of your work, it's the Usonian houses I find the most inspiring and relevant to me. This democratic idea of well-designed, mostly modular housing for and affordable by the masses. Henry Ford and the Model T in housing. You've managed to do this with the Prairie House. I've always wanted to do that with the Coastal House."

"So that's where we're going here? Holding to the idea that the democratic yearning can sustain you on the high seas of ambition? Henry Ford talks a good game. If we leave aside his disagreeable distaste of those of the Jewish faith. He treats his workers as human beings, with dignity. Unusually enlightened for the times I must say. My Usonian houses, now. In concept, democratic. My critics disagree with the reality. Argue that I catered to well-heeled elites, not the masses, creating what in the end are very expensive houses."

"But don't we start with the ideal?"

He fixes me with a hard stare: "When did it occur to you that you could be a tribune of architectural idealism?"

I know he agrees with me. But this master won't let you up on the mountain with him unless you earn it, fight your way to the top.

So I show some fight: "A good friend, a mentor, once made the point that all culture ultimately comes from the poor. From peasants!"

"Ah, here it is: the hidden flame of your undying purpose. Although you'll have to explain yourself with…more clarity."

"Mr. Wright, you'll agree with me. We don't get our great art forms, say, the Delta blues, without West Africa, without the legacy and pain of slavery turned into something beautiful. Take Bartok's piano concertos. Would they exist without his study of Hungarian folk melodies and putting them in Modernism's blender? The great cuisines of France and Italy weren't developed in palaces but on farms. So many of history's greatest minds weren't sharpened on privilege but the lack of it."

"It's one slice of the pie, Brian, but not the only one when it comes to the origins of accomplishment. The premise I generally agree with. It's a question of how this motivates you."

"If we have some sympathy for the notion that the meek should and deserve to inherit the Earth, then the democratic ideal is a good orientation for an architect—to serve the many as best we can."

"Brian, you understand by now, painfully I'm sure, the realities of patronage in the practice and how it challenges our democratic yearnings. The need to work for people who can pay you. Of course, well-paying clients are not the enemy. You can produce great works with rich clients and why not? Now the academy: a pain in the *derriere*. But it has its democratic purpose I suppose. I have my own school, and you have had yours at your Ghost world, to address the responsibility—tedious, at times—of midwifing architects to society. Yes, we do take everything we've learned, as architects, and can apply it to the grander democratic vision. I have tried to climb that mountain, too…"

He thinks for a moment, then continues. "In our stubbornly philistine culture, yours and mine, we have yet to create an architecture, a building tradition, that truly brings to life what it means to be a democracy. I have tilted at that windmill since before you were born. At times, I am not fully sure what it has done for me, or what I have done for democracy. Not enough I will venture. But I am only one man in my time, and so are you, in your time. Now: what have you done, Brian?"

If he can leave the question not fully answered, so can I.

We emerge into brutal sunlight at the end of the walkway, where there's another petroglyph-inscribed boulder. We pause for an instant, and turn back under the protection of the heavy pergola crossbeams and head back to the main pavilion.

"Brian, we have both adopted an ethical rationale to justify things we have a hard time admitting to ourselves. We make excessive demands upon the world, our loved ones, our clients and patrons, our mentors, too. Our bankers. We create complexity in our relations by our professional selfishness. In the name of democracy, at times. Which may be a genuine impulse—of course it is—but it is also a flag-of-convenience for the larger idea that you and I were put on this Earth for one reason, mainly: *to build*. Culture may come from the poor, but not budgets. You do understand that if you stick to your principles, you are not going to build very much."

"Mr. Wright, you have built nearly eight hundred buildings."

He pins me with an Olympian stare, haughty in its silent rebuttal, for putting *his* legacy into the conversation with my ambitions. The self-described world's greatest architect is having none of that. He also did not warm to the implication that, just maybe, he's compromised his integrity at times. Zeus was an all-seeing god, wise beyond mere human comprehension, but could be murderously vindictive.

"Mr. Wright, I didn't mean to suggest..."

Allowing that statement to trail into wordless apology calms him. His Minotaur-sized ego retreats into its cognitive den.

"Brian, this peasant logic. All well and good. But mastering the three chords of the blues is not enough to take you where you want to go from here. You'll have to push yourself in new directions, and risk it all. You might start with more attention to craft. This might seem—what do the Communists say—bourgeois. A fetish. This protests far too much, Brian. If you're devoted to democracy, it's equally important the front door and kitchen gets as much attention as the floor plan."

An instant fever storms across my forehead, then races up and down my spine. I say nothing out of respect.

A spiny lizard scuttles into view and arrests its progress at our feet. This tiny, colorfully flecked monster is no longer than a drafting pencil, *scelaporus magister*, with scales of gold, green, tangerine. Utterly still, it faces us down, blocking the way forward.

Wright, amused, turns to me, and in a whisper says, "I don't like intellectuals, Brian. Because they are superficial, operating from the top down, not from the ground up. I've always flattered myself that what I represented was from the ground up. It doesn't mean we don't intellectualize, as a necessary evil, but you get my point."

"It's always better to be good at doing rather than talking."

"If you really believe in something, Brian, as you do, that something will happen for you. The price you pay—the compromises you make—is another matter."

Then he disappears into the sanctuary, leaving me to muddle back out into the desert, into another mirage field, embraced by light bending through the scorched air.

The Angel: Beulah Oxner

Sunlight bleeds down upon her scrawny shoulders through cracks between the gable boards overhead. We're in the attic of the shed in our barnyard, now renovated into a bedroom and clubhouse for our two young daughters. We're sitting down, facing one another: Beulah on one white-painted iron bedstead, me on the other.

"No, Brian, this was never a chicken house," she says firmly.

"There was chicken shit on the floor. What about the little flap door, down there, not a foot high? Could only be for chickens."

"No, there was never chickens here," she says, smiling now.

"I guess we'll just agree to disagree."

We fall into silence, a joyful pause in a joyful relationship.

Beulah, the village matriarch, is our next-door neighbor, a resident here in Upper Kingsburg for decades. She's about eighty now, widowed from Albert several years, but not yet afflicted with pancreatic cancer that will take her soon. Sitting there bathed in morning light, she bounces ever so slightly on the bed, her feet not touching the floor, swinging back and forth. I get the sense she's drifting from me.

"Oh I lived in attics and cellars a fair bit as a young girl, going from one house to the next, where the work was, you know, where they sent me. They weren't the warmest places, I'll tell you that, and sometime at night when everyone was in bed, dead to the world, in the winter, I'd come down in my nightgown and the blankets piled on me and lie down right by the wood stove. Any wonder I never caught fire!"

In the stillness of the moment, I feel like I've been transported to a chapel where suddenly a celestial being has materialized with wisdom from a world beyond the earthly.

All I can do is nod, and listen, knowing I'm privileged to be on this journey into the deathless past with her. Beulah was orphaned at three, lost her mother to Spanish flu, and raised by relatives in Rose Bay, down the road from here, until she was old enough to be rented out as a domestic servant to families across the community. And as she recalls those days and what it was like to be a young girl, motherless, working from dawn to dusk, sometimes only for room and board, I really do hear and see Beulah transformed before me into a young girl.

We've known Beulah over a decade now but it feels like she's been a part of our lives forever. Beulah and Albert were much like grandparents to our children, funding their first bank accounts with five-dollar gifts, and ensuring there was always a small bag of toys for each child when they came over to their house for a slice of rhubarb or blueberry pie. Their neighborly spirit was exactly what we were looking for when we bought our farm. In the early years, as we fixed up the property, Beulah was always an affectionate, helpful presence. Nothing pretentious about her. She had a connoisseur's appreciation for the fake drama of the "wrasslin" show on TV every Saturday, her and Albert's favorite when he was alive. She knows when Marilyn and I get up in the morning, noting it in her diary. Even today she lives mostly outdoors, picking berries, working her garden. Often we see her sitting in a field, literally doing the splits, always being productive, always a smile for us. A small woman with a huge presence. And yet here she is, gone into her past, speaking from the soul of a young girl with her life in front of her, in the body of a woman with her life mostly behind her.

As an architect, it's pretty unfashionable to talk about soul.

How does a building—or just a simple room—acquire soul? How can a shack of boards and shingles become a time machine? A device for magical experiences and transformations? How does a shack turn into a temple? Is it possible, truly, to build spaces in the present that summon spirits from the past?

There's nothing in my formal education as an architect that teaches that. If I'm capable of investing anything with soul, I'm sure it relates to knowing people like Beulah and trying, genuinely, to connect with their dreams and the realities of their histories and what they desire to experience in stepping under a lintel, or walking across a barnyard, each arm burdened with a pail of wild raspberries.

Years later, during a community party following one of our Ghost projects, we'll hold a wake for Beulah. People will read poetry they've written about her. We'll project photographs of her. We'll tell stories about her as the drinks flow and the fog rolls in that night.

Holding a wake for the village matriarch, especially when you're a newcomer in the community, is risky. But I'll risk the criticism from the people who've lived here all their lives. Even so I'm still relieved that no one comes knocking at my door with complaints afterwards.

As a young girl, Beulah lived and worked in our SkyRoom when it still had a house above it. She pickled food and bottled jams there. She worked like a slave in the cellar but wasn't destroyed by that. Because here she is, in our chicken house that she says never had chickens, an angel who turns the past into the here and now.

The Modernist: Mies van der Rohe

Standing at the bottom of the staircase chiseled into this massive travertine plinth, I'm conscious of the need to silence my mind and the critic in me (an occupational hazard) who knows so much about this building. Although describing the Barcelona Pavilion as a building is insufficient. It's that rare convergence of architecture and art, all poetry in its proportions, perceptual effects and structural inventiveness.

To experience the Pavilion as Mies intended requires a willingness, even a vulnerability, to be intuitively led forward, sideways, and backwards at times, by the kinetic geometry and pinwheeling relationships in this well-tuned architectural instrument. It's a structure, *the* structure, that best exemplifies the Modernist grammar that I absorbed as a young architect and still value, nearly a century after the Pavilion was built as Weimar Germany's showpiece exhibit in the 1929 International Exhibition in Barcelona.

A half dozen steps up to the plinth surface reveals the long, rectangular reflecting pool ahead, bordered at the back by a creamy travertine wall, scaled to human height, that runs the width of the plinth. The pool, which reads as a black void, covers most of a plaza moving inward from my left. To the right of the pool, there's a slim expanse of travertine plaza, bordered by another travertine wall and a long bench, also travertine, where Mies sits in three-quarter profile from my vantage point. He's a large man in a dark suit, a lit cigar in hand. Must be in his seventies, mostly bald, the features on his face drooping with basset-hound sadness. He stares balefully across the plaza, an unmoving presence until a vigorous plume of smoke escapes him, colonizing the air above the pool. It occurs to me that he's not merely exhaling, but experimenting for my benefit with another diaphanous, optical effect in a structure designed around a celebration of such effects.

I could walk over to Mies in a few seconds but, behind me to my right, under the famous low roof that floats over me, I'm drawn to a corridor leading inside. The corridor is formed by a green marble wall on the interior and a translucent glass wall on the outside.

I tell myself that approaching Mies should be done through the demands on my sensibility made by the Pavilion. It's the space created by the man that needs attention first, not the man.

I wander into a reception area past a free-standing golden onyx wall on one side and a glass wall on the other that's shrouded in a red curtain, crossing a rectangle of black carpet, another void. I'm reminded that the colors here—gold, black and red—the colors of the German flag—are the only direct references to the patron, otherwise the Pavilion speaks exclusively in the language of architectural experience.

I keep moving forward, drawn towards a roofless terrace at the rear, screened from the inside by panels of light-green glass, and featuring another, much smaller reflection pool, bracketed by end walls of green Tinos marble.

Here I'm confronted with the perceptual ambiguities I've long wondered about. Every site line is specific, controlled. But the effect is far from rigid, or reductively symmetrical, but dynamic, in balance, without being repetitive or chaotic. Everything's poised but in motion, that's how it works on you. Because of how the luxurious materials—glass, polished marble, chromium-plated steel columns, pooled water—combine with light and shadow, your eyes are compelled to negotiate overlapping veils of reflective surfaces, creating an ever-mutating perceptual reality. You're in a constant state of surprise about where you are and what you're seeing. Just when you think you're entering an actual room, a factual interior, the space deconstructs on you, bringing the outside in from openings and vistas above or beyond you, or both.

I thoughtlessly submit to the maze of planes—a labyrinth, in spirit—made of free-standing walls and glass partitions and the openings between them. This is a master class in the concept of *the reveal*—the withholding of views, keeping you in suspense, until you absolutely need to experience whatever needs to be revealed.

For some visitors, this version of the free plan under a floating roof must be maddening, confusing. Where's inside? Where's outside? Is there a facade? No? What's the point of all this?

For an architect the point is pretty obvious: this isn't a building for habitation in a literal sense. It's an experimental work that, as Huxley said in a different context, opens the doors of perception about what is possible, and desirable. Knowing myself how the free plan legacy liberated the architect, this stroll under the roof feels like entering the inner sanctum of an epoch-changing inspiration.

So often, as architects, we turn ourselves into knots, trying to calibrate effects to satisfy a design objective and then find ourselves fighting clients, budgets and zoning. Here, in a world far removed from these pragmatic concerns, Mies has conjured up the Platonic ideal for how space should be designed and experienced. Modernism at its most lyrical, guiding us how to see, how to move, and, ultimately how to be.

At the far end of the rear garden, in a corner of the reflecting pool, hovers the George Kolbe sculpture, *Morgen*, a nude goddess, youthfully sensual, a green-tinged bronze that blends with the marble behind it while three-dimensionally apart, hands over her face, as if shielding herself from incoming light. It's an odd choice. In the 1920s, Brancusi, the Cubists and others were achieving in advanced art what Mies was doing in his field: inventing a Modernist language that exploded representational ways of seeing and explored the possibilities in abstraction. So what Mies chose for a sculptural work (working with Lily Reich, the designer who collaborated with him in creating the Barcelona Chair first deployed in the Pavilion) is relatively old-fashioned. The work introduces a strange sentimental note that to my mind speaks to an unresolved conflict under the surface of the design brief.

Mies had been commissioned to create a building to bring alive the optimistic spirit of the "new Germany" in recovery from the tragedy of the First World War. The Pavilion would—and does—create an experience in support of the values of democratic openness, transparency, cultural progressiveness, technological innovation. The sculpture isn't an affront to that, but it does echo something older in its representational earnestness, a nod perhaps to the conservative or authoritarian impulses roiling beneath the well-intentioned surface liberalism of the Weimar worldview that would eventually corrupt into the embrace of men like Hitler. Or, just as likely, the bronze could be a link to the Classical canon, although more Hellenistic than Hellenic.

It's at this point, contemplating the statue, that I swivel around and, at a short distance beyond the end of a corridor, on the plaza, I now see Mies now staring at me, but otherwise in full profile in his repose on the long travertine bench. The instant I start my approach, he turns away, inhales from his cigar, and waits for me as if he's been sitting there for the proverbial hundred years of solitude.

Exiting the corridor into Spanish daylight I turn back and there again, following me, is the low-hanging concrete roof. One critic said the eight chrome-plated cruciform columns inside the building core aren't so much holding the roof up but struggling to keep it from floating away. My sense of the roof being on the move, sliding over partitions within the open-ended interior, sometimes only half doing so, is one of the forces here that illustrate how energetic and active the space is, here in this playground of tectonic fluidity. Mies denies De Stijl influences, but it's hard not to see, in plan, an early all-over Mondrian grid where planes intersect and extend in abstract space, much as they do in *Pier and Ocean*, a painting from 1915.

"There is so much here," I say, tentatively.

"And yet, there is *almost nothing*," comes the reply in German-accented English, his voice gravelly from a lifetime of cigars.

"Less is—"

"—more, of course, but not always," he interjects. "Peter Behrens said this, but I'm happy to have appropriated the axiom. Good artists borrow. And great ones? The bigger problem of architecture is achieving quality through proportions, and proportions cost nothing. Quality is about the proportions among things, not the things themselves."

I'm about to tell him that I was once a visiting professor at the Peter Behrens School of Architecture in Dusseldorf—but before I get the words out, he has a terrible coughing fit. He's not a well man. While he settles himself down, I take the opportunity to direct the conversation. "I understand the design principles at work here, how you exploded the box, which links you to Wright, breaking free of established or authoritarian structure, allowing the energy of something bigger to come inside, the celebration of the democratic spirit, opening the world up, but also speaking to the landscape, nature."

He eyes me, skeptically. I have no sense of the inner man here.

So I try again: "I think what gives the Pavilion so much power is how you've been able to bring together the monumental, the weight of the plinth, the stereotomic, with the lightness of the elemental, the tectonic flexibility of the planes, on top, the house of cards that create all these intriguing spaces...and spaces in between."

Absorbing this comment requires from Mies a drag on the cigar.

"There were obvious priorities to manage," he says dismissively. "As for Wright, he is a great architect. We spent many enjoyable hours together at his Taliesin. He cherished freedom! And built a kingdom!"

I'm missing some vital entry into the conversation.

"Look, behind you, on the roof," he barks.

I do. A tiny black head. A bird playing peek-a-boo with us. Head appearing, disappearing, re-appearing.

"He has been playing this game for a while now," Mies says. "I'm sure he has a different concept of space than we do. More pragmatic. A place to hide, to base his attacks for food, to raise a family."

"It's a raven. A young one."

"Unusual here, but not unknown."

We let that sit with us until—

Mies: "Ravens are among the most playful of birds. They have been observed sliding down snowbanks in Germany. Quite acrobatic. They are, and correct my impression if you understand otherwise, among one of the few wild animals who make their own toys. Breaking twigs from trees to play with."

He's affecting an avuncular benevolence here, trying to engage or co-opt me, and set me up for a point to be made, inevitably, a few comments down the road from here. I'm not fooled. Behind the heavy-lidded gaze, within the pungent halo of cigar smoke, there's self-absorption, single-mindedness. I can tell he's only interested in a conversation about architecture. His architecture.

"And the lesson of the raven is?" I ask.

"Well, beyond the larger ideologies at work here in the Pavilion, both political and architectural, we must argue for the gentler, playful aspect of humanity, too, also universal. Poetry is serious by definition, a refined art form at its best, but within its forms, the forms we build, there can be lightness, uncertainty, humor, a game that keeps our senses entertained if not our conscious minds. What finally is beauty? Certainly nothing that can be calculated or measured. It is always something imponderable, something that lies between things."

"The presence of the marble here can certainly be calculated."

"You may know my father was a stone mason, and I passed my youth in his *atelier*. So you might say I have honored him here. Yet in a way there is emasculation, too. For as you can see, clearly, the monumentality and weight of stone is of no more consequence—or heavier—than sun-dappled water reflected in the underside of a roof. You might well ask: what is more solid?"

There's something about the allusive way he's talking that causes me to walk away toward the reflecting pool and, once there, my back to him, to make a point of staring in silence into its shallowness that conveys so much depth. Turning back to him, I say, "If you had to convey one lesson this building teaches, what would it be?"

"Architecture should be rooted in functional considerations, but it can reach up through all degrees of value to the highest sphere of spiritual existence into the realm of pure art. That is the attempt here. It is art to define the idea that we need an architecture that explains how in our world, there are no absolutes, not in structures, not in human relations, nor in the Self. We are largely mysteries to ourselves and others. In this fractured world, all we have is perception in its changing forms. The game is to be responsive to this reality."

"Which leads us where?"

"Without access to perception in its complex diversity, there can be no knowledge gained. We must move through perception toward knowledge, not the other way around."

I have an impulse to skip flat stones across the pool to disturb the illusion of tranquility here. It isn't so much that I'm frustrated but approaching Mies here feels like a journey through his Pavilion: he's a labyrinth as a man, as a thinker. I suspect the deeper one investigates Mies, the more unstable your point of view becomes. He's as paradoxical and enigmatic as his best work, a montage of contradictory

163

impressions. You don't impose meaning on a labyrinth a priori. You experience the labyrinth firsthand, that's how meaning is created. While Mies is the exemplar of the International Style, its grammarian, his brilliance here surpasses any style. It has a romantic quality. For a building that worships the hardness of technology and engineering innovation, it's so sensual. This cannot be said of all his work, not the later skyscrapers, and certainly not the work of his imitators who have populated our skyline with banal steel-and-glass towers.

The postmodernists thought they'd demolished him, saying less is a bore. His work outlives their critique.

He sees that I'm wrestling with his rhetorical gamesmanship.

"Mr. MacKay-Lyons, are we in agreement that we are conducting our friendly interrogation here in a garden, a landscape of a kind, a grove, filtered through the medium of industrial logic, and technology? Is that not the goal of all architects: to resolve, even heighten our relationship to the natural world, in one form or another?"

"It's an element in your grammar that I wish—"

And now he leaps at me—conversationally speaking—following an exuberant exhalation of smoke that speaks to the inferno inside this man who nonetheless looks like he could expire any minute.

"Grammar! Indeed, the boundary conditions, the limits. It is one thing to create a grammar, if not exactly by accident, then as byproduct, as result of something else entirely. Grammar! Yes, one does not invent one overnight. This is the work of a lifetime. Should one be fortunate enough to create a language, what is the ultimate responsibility? Surely you see it in every gesture that surrounds us?"

This is a test.

He says, "To *know* the rules..."

I nod in a way as to assure him—

"To know the rules, gives one the freedom to..."

We do understand one another, wordlessly.

The Farmer: Albert Oxner

In the doorway of the shed, he's sitting by himself on a paint-spattered wooden chair, an old man in old work clothes. He's fileting a feed of mackerel for us while chewing tobacco, his face half in shadow from the angle of the sun turning to sunset.

"Brian, come down and sit a piece and we'll yarn a spell."

I sit on the edge of the stoop, watching him as we talk about the weather. I sense in his subtle questions that he knows something's not right with me that needs straightening out. Until this moment I wasn't conscious of that myself. I guess he'd been watching me stomp around our field lately, visibly crestfallen that the deer have once again defeated our fences and chewed up more of the orchard.

Albert, the village patriarch, knows what's wrong and it isn't my failure to deal with the persistence of the deer. It's that I'm wearing my impatience with the facts of nature as a crown of self-importance. And so, we yarn about that for a spell during which Albert, employing a folksy Socratic technique, probes me in ways that allow me to see for myself that there's more patience I need to cultivate if I want to become more than a failing weekend farmer. To tweak a few of my psychological knobs, he didn't rely on any certification as a life coach. The man can neither read nor write, never attended school.

"It all takes time, Brian," he says.

As modest as the man is, there's something regal about him when's he surveying the world from the doorway of the shed, the entrance to his throne room, as I like to think of it. He can see who's coming up the road and decide whether he'll retreat into the shadows or step fully into the light, announce his presence, and as he's done with me, share the wisdom of his experience he'd consider a duty as much as a pleasure.

The shed is nothing special, tools, a work bench, a huge vice grip, a wall of stacked slab wood, essentially lumber waste, the most economical heating fuel for the stove. The shed smells of fifty years of toil as a farmer, inshore fisherman and winter woodsman.

"The kids, they got something going on in the city this weekend?" he asks, as if it isn't a matter of concern. But it is. "I guess there are things to do in the city, more than around here for the youngsters."

He and Beulah love being around our three children and treat them like their own. He knows they have lives ahead that will be totally alien to him, yet he's proud of every step they take, even their mistakes. He misses spoiling them, taking them for rides in the ox cart. This man is a king in my world here for many reasons, and it's not because of any money he's saved that he cares nothing about. (In a year from now, after he's buried, a victim of barn emphysema, or farmer's lung, they'll find a sock hidden under his bed, stuffed with paper money so old it's no longer legal tender.) Albert is a king to me because he truly has his own domain, his land, and over the decades he's cultivated it sustainably, feeding his family, selling or trading his small surpluses at market, meanwhile leaving a small piece of the world a better place.

From Albert I learned to see and appreciate the design virtues of the traditional barnyard, how the strategic placement of simple farm buildings, based on one's knowledge of the climate and weather patterns, could create microclimates and protected spaces that made daily life pleasant and work productive. His was a classroom alive with what it means, fundamentally, to survive. Albert loved animals deeply, wouldn't hurt never mind kill the peskiest of raccoons and porcupines eating at his garden or stripping the bark from trees around here. But at times he found himself required to slit the throat of an aged or infirm ox that worked his field and was much more than a farm asset, or a pet, but a close friend. He lived a code of ethics that if more of us adopted, we'd be living in a different world than the one that exists, where despite the growth and scale of our food system, we're arguably less healthy, so many millions of us nutritionally deficient in ways that breed chronic illness. If we followed the lessons of Albert's life, we'd likely still kill and eat animals, but we wouldn't cage them in animal concentration camps and force-feed them to slaughter.

166

Self-sufficiency and sustainability were the guiding values in the culture he grew up in. They wasted nothing. Made everything: tools, furniture, food, entertainment. Electricity and pavement only arrived here in the 70s. For Albert and his neighbors work was a holiday. They enjoyed what they did, otherwise it would have been a very long life. Their enjoyment didn't come without pain. One day, Albert, working alone, was with his cattle grazing over at Shobac when one kicked him, broke his leg. So he crawled his way home over the hill, which took hours. No iPhone to call 911. No phone at all.

"I'm thinking, this year I'm gonna re-shingle the barn, Albert."

"Is that right?"

"If the money's there, yes."

He looks off, summoning something. So I wait.

"One morning when I was young, my Dad and I decided to change our barn around. It used to be double boarded up and down between the heavy timbers but it got rotten from the weather. We stripped off the double-boarding, and we put studs between the old timbers. Then we covered them with horizontal boards across. On this we put the shingles. We then took the oil from the livers of cod we caught and mixed it up with iron-oxide powder and ox blood. This we painted on the shingles. When we put a drop on a shingle one night, by the next day it would soak right through to the other side. I'll tell you, Brian, it was some stuff to make the shingles last."

The story of Albert's barn renovation relates to a major shift in construction from a heavy-timber system brought from Europe to a light timber one that emerged here over two hundred and fifty years ago. Albert and his Dad were modern, engaged in a pragmatic search for better building practices responsive to their climate and the available materials locally. Their recipe for curing shingles highlights an ethos about innovation—or experimentation—disciplined by the awareness that whatever you did, you couldn't get things wrong. Or you could find yourself without food, or with a roofless house after a storm, or your animals refusing to work. Albert's oxen were not only trained to work but he taught them to plough the fields on their own.

The last time Marilyn and I saw him was at the hospital. I knew this would be the last time we'd be together.

"After 80 years, Brian, you're living on borrowed time," he said, initiating one of the quietest silences in my life.

Sitting there I saw Albert slipping into the shadows, going through another doorway, but still and always a king in my eyes, the wise elder, and patient even then as he waited for darkness.

The Mystic: Louis Kahn

Walking towards the south portico that leads to the front entrance, my head down to protect myself from the Texas sun, it occurs to me that the best and perhaps only way to approach Louis Kahn's work is obliquely, from the side. The Kimbell Museum presents itself like a ship's broadside, gangways left and right, front and back, that lead to multiple entrances without demanding you submit to the classic frontal symmetry of a Palladian facade of the kind that Kahn's early mentor, the French architect Paul Phillippe Cret, imposed on some masterful public buildings in Washington, including the Federal Reserve.

167

There's a democratic idea here about accessibility when you can enter a building from multiple points of view.

As I crunch forward on a travertine gravel path, the echo of freeway traffic in the distance fading, I have before me the quiet but imposing flank of the building in elevation, revealing its tartan grid pattern that Kahn if not invented, then reinvented: the modular assembly in eloquent proportions of six "thick" cycloid vaults, clad in travertine, with an equal number of "thin" boxy spacer-structures woven in between. Each time I come here I find myself wondering whether I'm looking at a building of my time and place, or a two-thousand-year-old Roman bath in North Africa, or a pasha's mausoleum in Constantinople. You feed on the evocation of the timeless here where the universal is local. This is a very definite building from indefinitely deep architectural roots that cross eras and cultures.

As I step through the intense stillness of the dry heat, another reason for the oblique approach comes to mind. Kahn is not an architect you face head-on, or look directly in the eye, not in my view. If you enter into a dialogue with his work, or look into its depths for too long, even with admiration, you'll find yourself blinded by its mystic presumption, fatigued by the distance he insists on you traveling to the origins of his originality. Kahn was obsessed with Scottish tower houses in rugged out-of-the way places, like the Broch roundhouses dating to the Iron Age. Where else does his Exeter Library come from?

Where I feel a strong connection to Kahn is in our shared belief in the inspiration of the *ruin*, the fragmentary record infused with the spiritual weight of history. My friend Robert McCarter, the distinguished architectural historian, wrote that during Kahn's year in Europe on a sojourn at the American Academy in Rome, he came to a decision to reject some elements of the emerging Modernist orthodoxy for building with thin materials. Instead he would devote himself to heavy and thick structural materials—the material of classical ruins. On that trip, Kahn produced exuberant watercolors of Egyptian pyramids and Greek temples that transformed ruins into volumes of blazing light.

As I close in on the south portico—which is an "empty" vault open on both ends—there are two celebrated sentinels of Modern art that reinforce some aspects of Kahn's intention here. On my left, nestled at the centre of a cruciform hedge, is Henry Moore's *Figure in A Shelter*, a large bronze on a circular plinth, constructed as a helmet-shaped form in two parts that provide over-arching protection to an abstracted female torso. It speaks to the primordial, the womb as the source of everything, and the universal human need for shelter. On my right, Isamu Noguchi's sunken sculpture garden, a rectangular green lawn abutting the basement level on which four large basalt stones of varying sizes exist in quietly intense spatial relationships to one another, each sovereign but connected. The abstraction of an archeological dig here suggests the aftermath of a mysterious discovery, like the scene in *2001: A Space Odyssey* where explorers on the moon surround a floating monolith at a mining quarry. Some say Noguchi came to love the ancient lunar quality of basalt because the moon was in the zeitgeist at the time, thanks to the Apollo missions in the 60s and 70s.

As I stride under the portico into the soaring embrace of the vaulted space, Kahn's version of a cathedral nave, the sensory equation mutates. The sound of water gurgling in the reflecting pool on my left rises up through the portico, then down over me. This sonic shadow forms its own womb. Here you know what it feels like to be, truly, a figure in a shelter. It's humbling, conveying what it means to be human, a temporal being under the aegis—and illusion—of something more powerful. And a connection to something beyond yourself.

I've arrived at the intersection of the portico and the courtyard of trees. It was designed into the scheme by landscape architect Harriet Pattison, also Kahn's lover, one of three women he was involved with at the same time. The courtyard is a transitional grid in which you're invited to slow down for a quieting moment of orientation. And so I move protected through dappled light until—suddenly—there's a glass curtain wall, the entrance, an abrupt welcome.

Inside I wander among the galleries, mesmerized as ever by the pearly grey light washing over the vaulted ceilings. It comes from the skylights, a thin opening running the length of each bay, hidden from below by wing-like aluminum brackets that reflect the light up against the concrete, and in the process transfiguring harsh Texas sun into something much softer—*heavenly*, which is a word to use sparingly.

Kahn and his clients wanted natural light to dominate the interior. Maybe that's why he opted to "trick" people at ground level into thinking the ceiling is an actual vault. In fact, it's two curved beams that don't meet at the top to allow the light in through the opening, a fact hidden from below by the brackets. The concrete loads come down on the end walls of the building on which the beams rest, not down through the vault, which is not a vault, engineering-wise. This violates an article of Modernist faith that says structure shouldn't be simulated, an appearance of real, but the real thing. Structure should reveal itself as it does in nature, as evidence of function, or, put plainly, as evidence of the truth of the world. Otherwise, what we have is mannerism: presenting the idea of something, not the thing itself. Whatever went into Kahn's decision-making with his engineers, the effect is nonetheless beautifully, calmly ethereal.

For Kahn, the light needed to be of a specific tone that, to paraphrase him, would suggest the powdery, silver-lavender wings of a moth. It's an amazingly intimate, peaceful environment to enjoy art. Kahn employed interior walls in the galleries—"served space" in his lexicon that so many of us have adopted—to create flexible, salon-like interiors while hiding the functional systems in the boxy spaces between—the "servant spaces." The experience of moving axially and across the grain in the procession of vaults all suggest to me a reference to the Great Mosque at Cordoba. Kahn had to have been there, had to, but if not in his lifetime, then before or after it—of that I'm sure.

Wherever you wander here in the Kimbell, no matter how big the crowd in your midst, you're bathed in Kahn's eerily comforting light-silence, a mutating nimbus of sensory calm. As I see it, Kahn isn't just an architect of structures. The Kimbell proves he's an architect of light. It's heresy to say this, but this building, while built to showcase and experience art, could exist as a work of art on its own—without the art!

I keep walking through the north galleries in a clockwise procession that eventually takes me into the south galleries where I find myself drawn to the diffuse rectangular light glowing from within the frosted glazing of the Penelope Courtyard. It's one of four garden spaces, subtracted from the vaulted bays, thus open to the sky as light wells, creating what J.B. Jackson calls "sacred groves"—for human-scale congregation and (for those so inclined) contemplation areas.

Pulling open the door, there he is, Louis Kahn, at the far end of the room, sitting on a travertine bench built into the walls. He's half in shadow, looking towards me, contemplating the Bourdelle sculpture on the plinth in front of me: *Penelope*, a Neoclassical bronze, attired in a pleated body-length robe.

Kahn, alone, is dressed how I expect him to be: a soft grey suit, a black bow tie over a white shirt, his mop of Warhol-esque white hair messily strewn about the head, the coke-bottle glasses in round black frames. It's the mature architect as man of the world, in the prime of life, a dash of the Ivy League professor in the mix.

I only know he's not a sculpture by subtle movements in the white cuffs peeking from the arms of his suit, and the small quiver in his hands, restless on his knees, with black smudges across the knuckles, likely from drawing with charcoal on tracing paper.

The scars from where the coals burnt his face as a boy in Estonia have faded into his skin, but they are still there. I once heard a good friend, a writer, suggest that Kahn's allegiance to travertine—a limestone that tends to scarring, to surface corrosion in slab from the gases escaping during formation—had something to do with his childhood injuries. I wouldn't link Kahn and travertine in that way but it's an interesting speculation. Kahn's insisted on leaving visible in his buildings the stress on materials that happens during construction—like the imprint of fasteners, or the wood grain in plywood concrete molds. Unlike the choice he made with the cycloid vaults, so called, he does want to tell us how things are built, what was involved, what the truth was in the construction process. It's an impulse I believe in.

"How accidental our existences are, how full of influence by circumstances," comes the slightly squeaky voice, each word clipped, enunciated, although I struggle to hear him over the water streaming through the horizontal channel of the travertine fountain that grows out of the sculptural plinth.

"I'm here because, I've always been here, I guess, and it's no accident," I say approaching him, coming into the sunlight that flows down through the canopy of ornamental trees in this small space, a twenty by twenty box that fits snugly inside one cycloid vault.

I sit beside him, just enough space between us. "There are so many things I'd like to talk to you about."

"In a small room one does not say what one does in a large one."

There's a challenge in that. So I say nothing for too long, but he's untroubled by the silence between us. "It's so hard to approach your work directly," I finally say. "That's the kind of effect it has on me, and the architects I've worked for who worked with you."

Charles Moore and Barton Myers, both mentors of mine, the latter the project architect for Kahn's Dhaka assembly hall, an important government building in Bangladesh, had stints in Kahn's practice and it shaped them, powerfully. I'm sure I would have been drawn to Kahn regardless, but it's interesting that I've come to Kahn through my mentors. It says something about how influences are really transmitted, in the dreams and whispers of people around the work.

"This idea of universality—of the timeless," I say. "Your work manifests it so deeply. I'm interested in the universal, but in a different context, for a world constructed of wood, in fishing shacks, barns, sheds. I'm curious what you make of Pevsner's contention that there's no connection between the basilica and the shed, the former being architecture, the latter being mere building. Says Pevsner."

He turns squarely to me. The effect is chilling at first, the gauzy stare through distortions of optical glass, but I feel genuine warmth, if not for me, then for the subject, and for conversation itself, a man who for all his mystic utterances famously loved a good gabfest with anyone with something to say– a cab driver, a street vendor, and the captains of industry who often paid his bills.

"I trust you're not Pevsner's biggest fan," he says, nearing a smile. "You know as well as I do that he probably spent too much time in Hampstead drawing rooms to have entertained a more enlightened view of where the meaning in architecture resides."

"I guess so but—"

And the professor in him needs to reinforce matters—

"I suppose Pevsner would say my bath house in Trenton is a 'mere' building" as you call it. Mere, from the Old French, I believe, means 'pure.' From Old Latin, it means 'unmixed.' I can live with that."

I smile, as if to say, clever, but diversionary. He concedes by continuing. "I've spent years sweating through my suits in the monsoons and marshes in the subcontinent, at Dhaka, bringing alive from modest means a grander story, a yearning for democracy, imposed partially from above, from local elites, true. But the forms I've raised there—the volumes, the spaces, the towers—speak to the poetic in everything and everyone, not just in every brick but everyone with a dream of something better. I don't see why a fishing shack or shed should lack poetry or universality. Everyone deserves a slice of sun, a square of natural light, a moment of silence in solitude."

"I'm trying to build a village by the sea with some of these virtues in mind. A fisherman's version of the Kimbell is what I'm after. A shrine not for high art, but something just as universal."

"A fisherman's version of the Kimbell?" That gets his attention. He places a finger to pursed lips, a signal for me to continue.

"Where I come from, you can walk around a fishing port and to some sensibilities, it's a random or chaotic clustering, thoughtless."

"Too much schooling will do that to an architect."

We both smile.

"I've seen so much *order* in the fishing ports and farms where I grew up. Communities with a kind of classical scheme, the structures in pinwheeling relationships to one another, and controlled geometries holding the larger plan together, indicating where the next building should be, without a need for the zoning bylaws to guide or restrict you. Visible integrity in how the purpose of a building—or an entire community for that matter—expresses itself. Not a basilica, but monumental, if a modest one. In wood, not concrete or brick."

During this little rant which he appears to enjoy, he assumes a variation on Rodin's Thinker's pose, leaning forward, elbow on knee, fist holding up his chin, a caring listener it seems to me. But clearly winding up to intervene with professorial exactitude.

"The classical order, Brian. The Greeks taught us that the column is where the light is not, and the space between where the light is."

"It's hard for some to feel the weight of light. How heavy it is."

"A room is not a room without natural light."

This brings us to silence—to the light right above us.

He looks up, squinting, then he's gone.

I'm now conscious of the water streaming through the channel in the plinth into the travertine basin. It's just me and Penelope, the long-suffering wife of Odysseus, a man lost to a lifetime of adventure.

In this solitary moment, I still feel part of an ongoing conversation with Kahn. It's not imaginary for me.

They say Kahn was nomadic, free of material obsessions other than what found its way into his practice. His home was his work and the human relationships orbiting around it, including his family, or his families, rather, were essential yet somehow peripheral.

He died alone in a train station washroom of a heart attack. It all sounds so lonely, his pursuit of the poetic and universal.

At the Salk Institute, another of his master works, the water channel through the main plaza empties in a basin towards the sea. It was written into the design scheme as a statement about the renewable source of human inspiration. Here, on more intimate terms, in this courtyard, the flowing water puts me in mind of the Castellian Spring at Delphi, where visitors cleansed themselves before consulting the oracle. And while I may not be on bended knee formally cleansing myself, I've come here, for this moment with Kahn, pure of heart.

My partner in our practice, Talbot Sweetapple, has a story about designing a house in the mountains of Cape Breton for a famous academic and his wife. The man was no fool. He'd been an orphan, then made good in the world, returning home to build a home on the road he grew up on. One evening at a dining room table, while reviewing the design, the guy says, my wife wants a white kitchen. Talbot says, Louis Kahn would never do that. And the guy says, with some outrage in his voice, I don't give a rat's ass about Kahn, he ain't never been to Cape Breton. At the next meeting, Talbot shows up with a drawing portfolio and there, at the same dining room table, he opens it up to reveal Kahn's sketches of Cape Breton.

174

The Hunter: Barnell Duffenais

"We were up in Cape Breton in the woods, hunting moose, November. We would have eaten just dandy had we bagged one but we didn't. Then the snow came hard, the arse dropping right out of the sky. My buddy, an older feller, says, 'Now, Barnell, if I die in my boots up here, how you gonna get me home? I looked right back and said, no worries, buddy, I'll just cut you up like a moose and haul you out.'"

Laughter explodes around the bonfire from our friends with us for Thanksgiving, all in thrall to Barnell, charmed by his roguish swagger, his appetite for the conversational limelight. In his middle sixties, Barnell shows signs of a life very well lived—but also a hard life, too.

In continuing his story, he tells of building-out a bivouac from spruce boughs, a shelter for him and his buddy in the storm. After that he goes around dusting snow off the ground, foraging edible berries most of us have never heard of, and finally comes across the gutted carcass of a recently killed moose. He gets down on his stomach and actually crawls into the dead animal and feels the heart and liver still there, and knows from the temperature and texture of the organs that they're good to eat. Soon, back at his makeshift camp, he's cooking up a stew with the meat and the berries, adding in some garlic he had with him. After the meal, the men settle in for the night.

"Jeez, sounds like an ordeal," I say, thinking that everyone else here, other than Barnell, would have died under the circumstances.

"Ordeal," he says, as if questioning my sanity. "Buddy, best vacation I ever had."

And once again, on this chilly night by the sea, our friends sipping strong nightcaps in bonfire light, all end up laughing.

I catch Barnell's eye. He loves this game and so do I.

What I've learned from my Métis friend about nature is all the proof I need in the validity of epigenetic theory: that knowledge and wisdom—our intuition about our deepest needs—can be passed on through our genes. Maybe it's why the Germans who move here like to settle in the woods. Why I need to be near the sea. If there's starvation in your history ten generations ago, maybe that's why, when you see food, you overeat. What Barnell knows about nature cannot be learned by one individual in the experience of a lifetime. No way. Some of his vast knowledge would need to be inherited, the insight in his blood from hundreds of generations of Indigenous culture, the hunter-gatherers here long before the Europeans. He can tell you what deer scat of a specific color means with the sophistication and clarity of an art critic. Why you should never hunt deer when they're eating leaves, but to wait until their diet changes to grass—that's if you don't want meat that tastes too waxy. He can tell whether the wood that built a fishing boat was logged at the right time in the moon's cycle based on how the boat sails in rough water. I've seen him on the beach, flat on his stomach, wriggling up to an otter just emerged from the dunes, going nose to nose with it, more or less convincing the animal that he, Barnell, is an otter himself. He seems to have walked out of an Ice Age glacier, bringing with him the brains to survive in the world, an aptitude most of us no longer have. Because of Barnell I've learned to see in ways I hadn't before.

As usual, tonight Barnell has dropped in unannounced, material-izing out of the woods where he's been hunting on his own, maybe for days, bringing in wild game to feed him and his extended family over the winter, and to barter with his friends for other things he needs, a muffler for the truck, tires for the Harley, maybe a jug of rum. He's always trading stuff, making the best of everything he can. Wasting nothing. Before the evening's out, he'll be handing me enough venison to fill a freezer. That's Barnell: generous, free-spirited, community-oriented. When I drop in at his place, he'll offer a hunk of turbot or a panfried scallop right off his fork. *Here, Brian, fill your boots.* He seems to have lived ten lives, raising multiple families, sailing the world as a master mariner, and always living off the land and sea. In the Acadian and Métis spirit, he's part of my extended family. He's been at the weddings of our children. And we do business together, his carpentry skills valued on projects around our farm.

Born and raised on the Port au Port peninsula of Newfoundland, home to a large Métis population, Barnell was one of thirteen children. If you know anything about isolated Métis communities, you know they led rugged lives. They lived on a boat in summer. In winter they were often on the move, hunting, living in teepees. He's experienced racism in Nova Scotia because of his Indigenous background, which I'll bet has eaten into his self-esteem. As tough as his life has been, he hasn't slept through it. He's had amazing experiences that he likes to share while we're mending fences together at our farm. Like the time a man died on a long scallop fishing voyage and they stored him in the forward prow. And because Barnell had the least seniority of all the men in the crew, he'd been assigned the crappy bunk under the for-ward prow and therefore had to sleep next to the corpse—for several nights! Now Barnell won't sleep on any boat. He tells of working shifts on one scallop boat, then, instead of going to bed, pulling alongside another boat, and jumping aboard to work another shift. Then moving to another boat. Working around the clock for days at a time.

As the evening ends, our guests all gone off to sleep, Barnell stands in his truck bed, handing down some choice cuts of deer meat, all care-fully wrapped. And then out he comes with a pail of fresh mussels for us. "Already had a good feed myself," he says.

I recall the last time I had mussels with Barnell when he was doing work on our boathouse. He was sitting down with his brother Vaughn by our pond, for lunch, steaming a pot of mussels over a small fire, the smoke blending with the fog on the stillest possible summer day. I suddenly had this vision of his Indigenous ancestors on this land— thousands of years ago—doing exactly the same thing.

The Environmentalist: Glenn Murcutt

At a cup-of-coffee past dawn, the historic town centre with its lack of history is slowly waking to a sunny breezeless day. We could be anywhere in the modern rural world. There's a global pizza chain outlet with loud signage flanked by a hair salon and a butcher. The local newspaper in the street box headlines a report about a crime spree linked to methamphetamine use by disaffected youth. On the corner, there's the stolidly imposing post office, cherished no doubt for its Victorian Italianate affectations, the inevitable clock tower, the three-bay arched masonry colonnade. There are probably a hundred of these post offices across Australia built from the same or similar plans.

177

Here in the rural heart of New South Wales, not far from the Tasman Sea coast, in a town first established to support the lumber trade, built on the flood plain of the Macleay River, the main story visible to me here is relentless adaptation to the consumer needs of the moment. Other than I expect that at the town museum, in sepia photographs under dusty glass, there'd be a fair bit about the eviction of Aboriginals from ancestral lands they'd lived on for thousands of years, and certainly plenty too on the history of the robber barons and colonial authorities who made out like bandits servicing the penal colony prisons that were the cultivating substance of this region so long ago.

I have nothing against commerce or communities like this. I'm from a region much like this on the other side of the world, where there's only grudging acknowledgement at best of our own dark history of colonial brutality. What I'm mindful of here this morning is how so many towns like this have become victims of a generic globalism that rarely takes into consideration what works best when building or adapting the structures people live and do business in.

There's now moistness thickening the air, the barometer dropping, along with the temperature. It's gotten sticky hot pretty fast. And clouds have arrived out of nowhere.

At the appointed moment, the open-cockpit jeep rumbles up to the post office. The driver is Glenn Murcutt, his balding head sheltered by a bush hat. After stopping near the curb, nearly on it, in fact, his stern gaze tilts owlishly at me over reading glasses that he never seems to take off in public. Suddenly, from my old friend, I get the big smile, alive with generosity and curiosity, the essence of this gentle, sweet man emerging from the aura of intensity that usually surrounds him.

"Get your backside in here," he says jovially.

Off we roar, up the street out of town and over the truss bridge spanning the Macleay that opens up luxurious views to an agrarian wonderland, the long vistas of green farm country around the winding blue of the river, a mountain range serenely in the distance, a lumpy sequence of dark pyramids against the sky. This is the kind of forgotten place that you might eagerly leave to make your fortune and, on a visit back, wonder why you left in the first place.

We're not talking above the engine drone, not yet. Neither looking at one another much. Just happy in each other's company. It's not like there isn't any communication between us. As a friend of mine once said, if you want something from a relationship with someone, you need to be traveling at the same speed they are. And right now, in this car barreling down the highway, we're doing just that.

At seventy-five, he's a little heavier and paler than the last time we got together at Shobac, where he's always an honored guest, basically family to us. Today there's a visible layer of suffering on his face, which is doubtless related to the recent death of his son, Nick, a non-smoker who succumbed at forty-six to lung cancer. Glenn temporarily shut down his practice—still, as always, a one-man show, no cellphone, no website—so that he could spend time caring for his dying son.

During that period Glenn and I talked periodically on the phone about what it means for a father to lose a son. It's weird but I'm aware of how difficult it will be, in person, to approach the same level of intimacy we had on a digital connection across ocean distances.

"What do you think, Glenn? A storm coming?"

He glances at me with playful verve, then looks around, head swiveling here and there. "There will be rain, but how fierce? How high are the birds flying, Brian? The frogs in the pond were quite loud last night, and before I left this morning, the spiders were all down from their webs. We'll have a downpour—look over there."

He nods toward a field where cattle are crouched together in a corner. Another marker of a coming storm he is wordlessly suggesting, assuming that I understand him. Shorthand between architects with a relatively obsessive interest in natural processes.

"It'll be a ferocious rain. The farmers need it in any case."

Among Glenn's gifts as an architect is that he's a climate expert of uncanny depth, partly the reason for his international renown after winning the Pritzker Prize in 2002. He's the world's leading critical regionalist. By that I mean he's an inspiration to a generation or two of architects striving to express universal architectural principles through the particularity of local building traditions, anchored by an inordinate sensitivity to ecology. Glenn is a master at blending a uniquely Australian vernacular, the stuff that works out here, within a dialect of contemporary Modernism that he first apprehended through the work of his early heroes, Mies, Le Corbusier, and the Finnish architect Alvar Aalto. Glenn's never built outside Australia and says he never will.

One critic said I'm the Glenn Murcutt of North America, a huge compliment. Glenn's work and his mentorship have influenced me greatly, although I'm wary in saying that too loudly or to the wrong people. So easily people misinterpret influences. When you are influenced, you're not always copying. You could be discovering something you already know is inside you. Before I knew who Glenn was, I knew climate and the environment—the impact of sun, moon, wind, all of nature in its infinite power and beauty—would be important in my work. But as a young architect, when I was first exposed to Glenn's thinking, a big window to future possibilities opened for me.

After twenty minutes or so, we turn off the highway onto a regional road that soon enough collapses into a rugged dirt track through a canopy of mature eucalyptus under which we bounce to a stop at the gate to his farm. Before I can jump out to open it—my responsibility as passenger—Glenn's leaps out ahead of me, whipping the gate to one side, beckoning me to get over into the driver's seat and bring the vehicle in, as if there isn't time or energy to spare. He did his job, now I do mine. Efficient in the first degree, he's always focused in his work on the most economical and collaborative solution. It reminds me of the time I drove Glenn and my son Matt to visit several of my houses in rural Nova Scotia and our truck slid deep into a ditch.

Glenn was outside instantly, figuring things out before the engine died down. Why the rush, I said. "Maybe in Canada, you can take your time," Glenn said in his no-bullshit way. "In the outback in Australia, at night, you'd be dead in a few hours."

His intensity is arguably the behavioral inheritance of his father who trained his children for life with militaristic verve. A father who took the family to live in the bush of Papua New Guinea while he prospected for gold in an area inhabited by a tribe of cannibalistic warriors. When they moved back to Australia, before dawn every day he would wake Glenn and his siblings and order them to run a half mile to the pool, then swim two miles before running home again, all on a stopwatch, all before breakfast and school, all on a schedule that only allowed for free time on Sunday afternoons. A father who made him, as a boy, read lengthy articles about architecture and quizzed him on them until he understood every last nuance.

As I know Glenn, he's sensitive to the human need in the moment and, in that regard, as he once said to me, more like his mother in emotional disposition. He's always quick to show he cares for you and your dreams. But there's principle engrained in his architectural ethics. Another time, in Nova Scotia, I took him to a house of mine that had won a boatload of awards. When Glenn walked in, he asked me where south was, wondering how the building would manage solar gain. When I told him the house was north facing, he walked right out. Wouldn't speak to me for the rest of the day. I love telling that story. Who else would you rather be in the foxhole with? Someone with principle, even when it hurts you (because it did hurt), or someone without it?

The Marie Short house is a five-minute hike across cattle pasture beyond a veil of trees swaying in the wind that keeps picking up. From here, the house looks like a run-of-the mill woolshed or industrial farm building that are all over the countryside here, its corrugated metal roof shining in a sunshine moment between the darkening clouds. As we approach through the field, you realize the house is two long narrow pavilions raised on wooden stilts, joined by a central corridor. Two buildings seemingly sliding past one another.

"Let's get a move on, Brian, or we'll be soaked to the bone," he says moving past me, looking skyward an instant before a blast of thunder, followed by the first rain drops. You'd think the man was a shaman, predicting to the minute, it seems, the storm's arrival.

We make it to the screened-in verandah of the south building as the deluge hits, the heavy rain beating on the metal roof with snare-drum intensity. Water whooshes loudly through the gutter down pipes into the funnels on the ground, recycling a valuable resource. His houses are famous for this kind of ecologically sensible design element.

Within minutes, as we stand there silently, the water starts to flood across the hardened land beneath the trimmed meadow. A large brown snake—a deadly creature—slithers in the water toward the house and goes right under us. That will make anyone weak in the legs. It's the scary difference between our Commonwealth countries. Canada has rattlers and grizzlies and Great Whites but, as a general assumption, we don't walk through the country, like they do in Australia, fearing venomous reptiles and scorpions, or trees with branches that bleed neurotoxins and sting for real when you walk into them.

"Rain patter on a roof, such beautiful music," he says, as if talking about a vintage wine, before walking into the open-plan living area by drawing back a section of glass wall to the interior. After he adjusts the blinds to let in much more light on a day that keeps darkening, he says, "I'll make us some tea, a plate of bruschetta. Sound good?"

He leaves me on the verandah, speechless again at where I am and how fortunate I feel to be here. Standing here inside a house that has long inspired me is like being invited by Bach to hear him play the Goldberg Variations on a harpsichord. Coming here again after all these years reminds me what I was put on this planet to do, thanks in part to Glenn bushwhacking the trail forward, eloquently and practically integrating climate and environment into everything he does. An architect for whom waste, and anything that can't be recycled or reused, ranks as a crime against our profession and indeed the world.

The house is a kit-of-parts, assembled out of cheap stuff, end-of-line wood stock and industrial components. His client wanted a home that could be taken apart and moved somewhere else if need be. For me, it's a genuine nod to the democratic ideal of affordability. No expensive chrome columns or concrete geometric forms or cathedral ceiling showstopper. It's a shed for living, raised on sticks in the spirit of Thoreauvian modesty. As Kahn said, what's important about the Magna Carta has nothing to do with the cost of ink. The idea is more important, and here the message is: you can make great spaces without big budgets. Air is free. And if anyone could be called the architect of air, in the way Kahn was the architect of light, it's Glenn.

Glenn has talked to me about the Marie Short house in different ways. I like his boat analogy best: where the air and light flow in the house—its climate—is controlled by the land-based equivalent to rudders and sails. The exterior walls of local timber, now weathered silver, are layered with glass and slat blinds that, depending on time of day or season, can be dialed in to bring in or restrict light and the breezes in each room, cooling or heating space as required. Glenn has designed exactly one building with air conditioning, no more. Many of his buildings are so finely tuned in manipulating climate that they don't have heating systems at all. It's a measure of his integrity and commitment to excellence—to doing the right thing—that the owner actually *willed* it to Glenn. In its modular elegance, the Marie Short house owes something by way of inspiration, I think, to the Eames House in California where I once spent a day with Charles Moore, talking to Ray Eames about the house she and her husband designed and built in the late 1940s.

182

I hear him next door, at the far end of the north-facing pavilion, the main house. Inside, he's sitting there absorbed in some drawings but strangely, no pencil in hand.

As I approach the table however I quickly realize the drawings are his son's work, including several tough-minded, off-the-grid cabins, the apple not falling far from the tree, the spirit of economy and sustainability running in the family.

"My son was an architect for twenty years," he says softly.

"He was a good one, Glenn."

"Yes, but an architect doesn't mature until his fifties."

"I'm still working on the maturity part."

And he smiles at my self-deprecating comment that breaks the sadness briefly. This isn't a conversation where we need to talk about Nick. Nothing more needs to be said beyond what is shared by the quality of the silence between us while looking at Nick's work together.

As day turns into night, the rain finally stops. Glenn opens up the connecting doors between the pavilions for cross-ventilation. It brings in the wonderful smell of fresh rain on the coolness of the night breeze.

"I'll say it again, Glenn, you've invented something here, a new form of building, and that's nearly impossible. The omnidirectional weather monitoring instrument. The climate panopticon. Observing and participating in the climate across all views."

"It is a simple building, Brian, for the simple but very deep needs we have as humans. I wouldn't make too much more of it."

Classic Glenn: deflecting praise.

"Far too modest."

"The panopticon was a term first applied to the guard tower of a prison. Is that how you feel about it? A prison?"

Mischievous Glenn.

"You know what I'm saying" I say, feigning irritation, while picking at the label on a sweating bottle of lager.

The breeze perks up, flowing gently through the space, lingering over the table, refreshing us but disturbing nothing else, not the drawings on the table that move so much inside Glenn.

183   *The Teacher: Essy Baniassad*

At the wheel of our car that's going far too fast on the highway through the Kalahari Desert, Essy still manages to perform in the cramped interior like a star on a big stage. He has a mime's skill for drama, his gestures and expressions alternating between subtle and exaggerated, his silences as interesting as his commentary. His voice and the language within it, a cosmopolitan instrument, is tuned with echoes of the Iranian boy who spoke Farsi and who, as a refugee from the Shah's regime, studied architecture in the UK and the United States where he learned English. It tells you, or tells my ears, here's a man who's seen the world and accumulated its wisdom.

"You know, when I meet students for the first time, I can see their horizons. I must say, for some, it's *terrifyingly close*!" Shoulders shrugging, mouth contorting into a visible frown. "They see too many barriers. Last week, one young fellow said, Professor, they won't let us do that. *They?* I said to him: Who are the *they? We are the they!*"

I grin but keep sketching as we race along, an hour from Botswana's capital, Gabarone. It was Essy who taught me to sketch in a fast-moving vehicle, like he's taught me so many things. Like how to think by taking on the ideologue in me, the young architect on a mission to improve the world. I listen to him as I don't others, drawn to his high-brow erudition. He's a bible of aphoristic insight clipped from the philosophical and literary canon, mixed with his low-brow pragmatism, the son of a brick mason, a fact I know he's quietly proud of. Essy maintains a restrained view of what architecture schools can accomplish. "In architecture there is much to learn but little to teach," he said one evening over drinks after a brutally inconsequential faculty meeting. "But what can be taught can be taught clearly." He has a low tolerance for theoretical bullshit but can speak it if need be. As dean of our architectural school in Halifax, a colleague who has done a lot to support my career, I've seen him in faculty meetings argue for a point of view, getting everyone in a lather, then spinning the table to argue the opposite position: playing chess with himself. For a man who can pass as the balding professor in wire-rimmed glasses, he's a virile force, fearless, capable of surfing out into the open Atlantic on his windsurfing rig or recovering from a gunshot in Peru that tore out half a lung.

Up ahead, a village behind the exit sign.

"Let's take a look," he says.

This is habitual on our travels, searching out signs of architectural life and history wherever we go. And here in Africa there are things to see. It's where the first human dwellings—outside the cave, that is—made their appearance so long ago now.

"Over there," I say, nodding toward a group of farm buildings, circular huts, rondevals, built with waub-and-daub walls—a hardened mixture of stone, dirt, dung and water—under conically thatched roofs. They look like giant mushrooms, connected to each other by stone fencing. We step out of the car next to a large green warning sign:

DISCLAIMER—THIS IS A WILDLIFE AREA—
YOU ARE STOPPING AT YOUR OWN RISK

Essy walks past the sign as if it doesn't exist. I'm not so confident but the site has my attention. Up close, it's clear the farm's been abandoned, the buildings all falling down. There's a For Sale sign on a metal post creaking in the breeze. Essy's nose is in the air, sniffing, his head swiveling, brain working. He's entranced by the decay. I see why. This is where the fact of human settlement began, when humans became bipeds going back millions of years ago.

For me, however, this scene is akin to coming across a corpse, evidence of a dead material culture.

"So gloomy, Brian, but of course I understand you."

"How could they let this place...die."

"A real farmer never sells the farm. But they are not you."

Essy once told me he's not an architect in the same way I am. He designs architectural curricula and builds teams of professors. He builds architects, not buildings. Essy, also unlike me, is a nomad, and anti-materialist to a fault. At his apartment in town, some of the frames on the walls don't have pictures in them. Does that signal rootlessness, the refugee from many years ago still on the run? Who am I to conclude that? He comes off as a very fulfilled individual. Curiosity overflows in him, along with a child-like playfulness. I once saw him on a Halifax street pick up a piece of string and spend an hour working it into different shapes, as if it were the greatest gift from the gods. The day after I graduated from architecture school, I was wandering in a daze through a downtown park, knowing it was time I had to think about my future while very uncertain of the next step. That's when Essy called out to me, and right then and there, took off his dress shoes and challenged me to a race in his sock feet. How fortunate I am to have a man with his sense of adventure in my life.

An hour later, we're all sweating in the airless office of the university president, where Essy has arrived to help set up an architectural program in partnership with our school in Halifax. Our host, formally dressed, and I suspect surprised by our informality, grows agitated, if quietly so, as the conversation unfolds.

"Forgive me, Professor," the university president says, interrupting Essy in mid-sentence. "We have nothing, no money, no resources, materials. How can we do this?"

"Do you have a shovel?"

A silent nod—

"What about dirt? A place to dig?"

Another nod.

"Then you can have the best architecture school in the world," Essy exclaims, clapping his hands.

Later, in the hotel bar as I wait for Essy to join me, I'm thinking about our meeting and the idea that architecture can grow out of nothing, out of limitations, from only the creativity in your hands, in the spaces built from digging holes in the ground. Can a hole in the ground be architecture? Well, it is at Shobac, in our granite foundations there.

When he sits down, I say: "Think he understood you?"

"I'm confident good things will come of this."

"How so?"

"This place may be poor in some financial respects. But so what, Brian? All culture comes from the poor, you know?"

The Entrepreneur: Donald Judd

In the sunset dryness of the high desert plains in southwest Texas, an hour's drive from Mexico, the landscape near Marfa imposes contemplative urges on you. As I follow the train tracks into town on foot, heading toward the cattle feed mill up ahead, I'm thinking how beautiful railway lines can be, the endless horizontal progression of wooden cross ties, nineteen inches apart, each impaled under perpendicular boundaries of steel that skate away toward some infinity beyond the vanishing point. I'm definitely not the first to feel that a railway line appears—in a place like this—as a mystical blend of the functional and the aesthetic. It works by intent towards a definably useful purpose but, with no trains in sight right now, it speaks to me as art. It puts me conveniently in mind about what's next, on my immediate right, past the wooden gate in the high adobe wall: the entrance into Donald Judd's world, his complex of buildings called The Block where he lives and works among the art he has installed there, mostly in two old airplane hangars bought from the U.S. military years back.

The Block is an entire city block in town. And yet, it's only a small part of Judd's inventory of buildings in and around Marfa that include several ranches and 40,000 acres of land. All this Judd acquired and renovated with the help of art foundations and by selling his own art to eager collectors worldwide. He has sort of singlehandedly turned Marfa—originally a sleepy railway town going back to the 1800s—into a global art mecca. Here you will find works by Judd and his peers from the art world of the 70s and 80s. Although Judd has long been grouped with the Minimalists, he rejects the label. Neither does he consider himself a sculptor, even though among his most famous works are

186

box-like forms in wood, galvanized metal, even concrete, built to be free-standing or as wall reliefs. Judd calls these works *specific objects*, a new three-dimensional art form, he argues, neither sculpture nor painting and created not as metaphorical devices or to represent anything but themselves. You see what you see. They are what they are. Judd intends for installations of his work here to be permanent, unlike, he argues, the practices of museum curators, gallery owners and collectors who move art around too often, or install things badly, or lacking context. Here the artists typically have their works installed in a grouping, according to their wishes, all towards creating the experience and conveying the meaning of the works as they think best.

Once I'm inside the gate, it's like entering a medieval courtyard from where a shogun and his retinue control and tax the surrounding territory, except what Judd has built or adapted here comes baked in the dusty vernacular of an American or Mexican border town that could (and has, at times) double as a Western movie set. At the other end of the complex are the two airplane hangars, built in the 30s, which are annotated with a line of clerestory windows under the gable, and together frame a courtyard about two hundred feet long and half that deep. The courtyard is formally defined by a U-shaped adobe wall inside the complex. Unlike the plumb exterior wall that goes right around the property on all sides, the walls of the interior courtyard follow the slope of the land itself. In the process Judd has framed space and created a microclimate. The courtyard is intimate, but feels large, a desert landscape in miniature. For me the contrast between the plumb exterior wall and the interior sloping wall elevates the courtyard into serious art without sacrificing architectural utility.

Judd emerges from under the pergola to my immediate left, a heavyset man, late fifties, a visible paunch, the long bushy hair nearly all grey, the beard too, and dressed as a gentleman farmer in a red plaid shirt, jeans, and scuffed cowboy boots.

"So it's an insult to your profession that I have the nerve to call myself an architect," he says softly but firmly. An audacious icebreaker. His manner doesn't feel fully confrontational, but he definitely wants to see what I'm made of. Not a small-talk kind of guy, and I identify with that. We're not men with hobbies. We don't play golf or collect coins.

"Don, you know as well as I do that art and architecture do not come from the same place, and involve much different processes, problems, ways of working, outcomes. Architects make terrible artists and vice versa, as a general assumption."

"That's rich, given what you say about the tragic state of architectural education. So hang me for not having a credential next to my name and membership in your club. You think all those acronyms next to your name mean something real? Have you speculated on the possibility that some minds have the dynamic range to shift between much different modes of production? Obviously, as an artist one cannot think like an architect. You need to step into your architect brain first."

I chuckle uneasily as he leads me toward the pergola, draped in grape vines, where on a long table of his design there's a liquor bottle, without a label, next to two small glasses. While he fills glasses for us, a single-malt whiskey, I take furtive glances around. Further to our left, a concrete lap pool. It's obvious the volume and proportions of the pergola and lap pool are related, and they also speak proportionally to the chicken coop and dog house to my right. Across the courtyard towards the major buildings, he's paid close attention to symmetry and proportion in his interventions. But I don't sense rigidity, either. And that has much to do with the concentric adobe walls that have turned the courtyard into a massive art work, a blend of art and architecture, yes, I have to admit. This place is a ruin, too, of a different kind, rehabilitated in practical but also poetic ways. What I've always liked about Judd is his sensitivity and allegiance to the pre-existing built environment. He considers it a moral imperative to fix up old barns or airplane hangars and storefronts rather than tear them down or spoil more land by building anew. We're on the same page there. It always saddens me to see a barn on its last legs, leaning toward oblivion, like an old boxer beaten by younger fists.

188

"I like your courtyard."

"Well if you are going to stray from symmetry, you'd better have a good reason."

He tells me offhandedly the adobe walls were built by two Mexican men from across the border, legally employed, brought in to do the job over several years.

"The practice of building with adobe has been entirely lost here and in much of Mexico, too," he says with melodramatic edginess.

"I know the problem, just different materials. Shingling a building in Eastern cedar back home was something everybody was brought up with and did, like learning to tie your shoelaces, shell a lobster, or take your grandmother to church on Sunday even when it bored you. But why learn anything from the past when there's plastic sliding?"

"Brian, the situation really is untenable. The neglect of adobe—even to Mexican-Americans who think it unstylish or un-American, not upwardly mobile, not middle class—indicates the larger problem."

"Go on, Don."

"My farming neighbors in Europe—I have a home there now I am renovating in Switzerland, in a quiet meadow—all have plastic dwarfs in front of their house. In Texas they use plastic ducks. All over the world there are plastic dwarfs and plastic ducks. It is possible that there are thirty million ducks in Texas alone...and don't get me started on plastic walnut paneling. All the classes love it."

The guy has an interesting sense of humor—all deadpan. I'm cautious with him all the same. He's shy, reserved, or courtly, like a retired sheriff who has seen too much ugliness out on the range, the bodies left to the vultures in the arroyos. But Judd's reputation and his essays also say: a difficult man, cranky about pretty much everything concerning the situation in art, given to fits of fury when drinking, and famously a collector of grievances against institutions, ideas, people.

"I take it you're not a big fan of contemporary architecture," I say.

He looks off, silent for too long, sipping his drink, giving me the impression he has better things to do. Turns out I'm wrong. Just ordering his thoughts. And now they flow out in that bluntly distilled, sardonic tone that I recognize from his essays.

"Most of the present beliefs should be dead beliefs, but contrary to my expectations, they'll take a thousand years to die. And then new stupidities will have filled the emptied space. That's where, if you're honest, architecture is today. Or most contemporary architecture. Take one of your mentors, Charles Moore."

I feel the heat rising in me.

"His whatever in New Orleans, Piazza d'Italia. A piazza? Well, the *clearing* among the skyscrapers, such as it is, this pseudo-ruin, this cut-out, this pop-up classicism, supposedly done to honor the local Italian American community? This assignment of classical ruins to Italian Americans is a typical and cynical misuse of history. It's history of the tourist brochure, of kids in fifth grade, of TV."

"Don, go ahead, cherry-pick at his work if that makes you happy. Moore was a very fine thinker, a real humanist with a deep sense of history. A great teacher. And he built some very good things. If you'd spent any time at Sea Ranch, you might think twice about driving a tractor through the man's reputation. And whether you like it or not, he's on to something, taking *his* potshots at the excesses of modernist functionalism, its coldness, and the religion that has become."

Slight nod, a touché acknowledgement, then:

"Now where *your* work is going, Brian, or where it could go, it is generally agreeable to me. You understand the relevance of 'regional'— not the crap of the postmodernists. An interest in the traditions of a region can be done right, and isn't incompatible with originality and—"

If I don't barge in, who knows how long he'll go on. So I do: "The Mexican poet, Octavio Paz, wrote: 'Taken alone, tradition stagnates and modernity vaporizes. When taken together, modernity breathes life into tradition, and tradition responds by providing depth and gravity.'"

He sips at his whiskey again, eyes narrowed to critical slits. "Let's agree the use of available materials is crucial, and that a building should not be an intrusion on the landscape or on existing buildings, which must be considered with respect and skepticism."

My turn to sip and order my thoughts. I'm not clear on how to engage. He's an essay in human form and that's fine, but I'm more interested in proof of concept.

"A good building is a good building, Don. For me it boils down to whether the result makes the world, even slightly, a better place."

He likes that a lot.

We stroll in agreeable silence toward the Quartermaster house, a small two-story building turned into a residence for himself and his two children who now live with him after their parents divorced. From there we move into the airplane hangars, and as we pause here and there to discuss his work as an architect, I see he has wonderfully fused his artist's conception of space with an architect's.

As we walk along, I sense he's in a constant struggle to keep his powder dry, to stop himself from haranguing into every conversational opening. Over time, candor mixed with anger, as he must know, wears on people. He strikes me as a man whose sensitivity unhappily shares space with the volatile ideologue impossible to shake from his positions. But I like people who talk to children as sentient beings, which he does with the young son of his Mexican housekeeper we meet along the way, engaging the boy in a conversation about art that would likely intimidate a college student. I'd like to think that when my children were young I treated them with that kind of respect when discussing matters of substance. You treat people seriously, they become serious people.

As we tour the complex, it hits me how much he has acquired. It's a mania. Navajo rugs, Indigenous art from the Northwest coast, Tlingit and Kwakiutl, furniture from classic designers, Rembrandt prints, the art of friends and peers. A house in Switzerland? A cast-iron building in SoHo? Some 40,000 acres out here? Marfa in total is a multi-pavilion, multi-location shrine to his work and his friends but also the art and artifacts of many cultures. And a library of 13,000 books.

191 Where does all the money from?

Now we're standing in an exhibition space in one hangar, entered through a four-paned glass pivot door that looks like something Murcutt would design to generate air flow, depending on wind direction.

"None of this was planned beforehand," he says. "Unlike my work, the situation was always fluid here, unknown to an extent. I am doing what makes sense in the logic of the moment. My vision here, as an emerging proposition, presents difficulties. Money being one."

"You have so much happening here, Don. You seem to be involved in everything. Art. Furniture. Architecture. It's an empire. I wish I had your business smarts. How will I pay for the things I know I want to do, and build, never mind the things I have yet to think of?"

"If you want to ask if I'm about to go bankrupt, come out with it."

Not so impressed with me but he continues: "There's a general condition of unpleasantness with money, in my business relations especially. Some collectors of my work collect because they love art. Too many are stupid self-invented big shots, collecting in wholesale to sell later. No respect for the art. Keeping it in storage. Showing it badly. So, because you need money, and I do, you can sell a collector a pair of trousers but not expecting he'll shit in them. But some will."

"Yes, but—"

"I am not going bankrupt, yet. But I buy too much. And it seems there's never enough money for the impulses eating at it."

"Debt has a way of causing problems, Don."

"Wright and Kahn, your heroes, dealt with it."

"Badly."

"I spend too much, it's true, but I'm not driving around here in a Ferrai or putting money into facelifts. I'm out here in the desert, making a place—a permanent home—for my work. Installed the way I want. Where the work can speak the way it was intended. And if possible, never moved again. If I don't protect my work, who will? You might ask yourself that question at your Shobac one day."

I notice yet another day bed in the corner here.

"There are beds all over the place here, Don."

"I need a place to think about and be with my work."

I see a man on the run, who won't be pinned down, feels hounded, sleeps in different places, as if he's the last man alive in a dying regime, moving between his bunkers to stay ahead of the assassins.

"You know where I sleep?" I ask. "In my barnyard, the attic of an old chicken shed. A box of shingles we cleaned up. For years my wife and I would escape the house, and the kids. Slept the sleep of the dead."

"I presume you're not partial to plastic ducks in your barnyard."

And he lets out a bellyache of a laugh.

Now we're standing in front of one of his vertical stack pieces: a column of gleaming stainless steel boxes, stacked one atop the other, the tops and bottoms in translucent plexi-glass, hiding nothing, signaling the virtue, literally, of unimpeded insight into its rectilinear spine. The space between each box is the same dimension as the boxes: positive and negative space given equal weighting in a vertical column projecting from the wall out three feet while appearing to climb it.

If I listen to Judd, this work isn't a metaphor for anything.

I'm not so sure.

I see the stacks as an existential staircase, a railway line to the sky and back, a device that suggests *journey*, forward and backwards, up and down, here and beyond, inside time and somehow beyond.

Try all you like to exclude metaphor, but it will find its back to you.

The Artist: Alex Colville

A pleasant spring afternoon at Shobac, the ocean horizon coming into view as we crest the hill and walk down into the valley toward the meadow that I've cleared among the trees.

Our journey feels orchestrated by unseen but sympathetic forces. We're a foursome silently on the move, a box of shifting proportions, with four human corners, each independent but moving together as an adaptive unit. I imagine us from above, looking down, the plan view, and see the space within our little group as a mobile courtyard fed with the goodwill of four people, all happy to be out here today.

I'm up front, with Alex to my right.

Marilyn and Rhoda, Alex's spouse, the pair behind us, are spaced as if they're matching the distance between the men ahead.

Everything perfect: the geometry connecting us below the sky-blue light, the ripple of incoming tide, the wind through the grass that seems to sway in sync with the strands of hair blowing across Marilyn's face.

I have this sense we're characters in a painting in Alex's mind.

One of Canada's most celebrated artists, Alex Colville, now about seventy, has been painting scenes like the one I'm describing for decades, inspired by the rugged drama and arresting beauty in the Nova Scotia landscape as the mythic backdrop to ordinary scenes of domestic and small-town life. The work itself is very far from ordinary, imbued as it always is with universal themes and what a Jungian would call the archetypal elements in the human story. He mostly paints what he sees on his walks with Rhoda through the farm land and country roads in the Wolfville area and along the levees, or dykes, built by Acadian settlers so long ago. Alex has been called, disparagingly, a realist, a representational painter, a mostly unfashionable distinction in today's art world. But what he paints isn't classic representation but the nuanced play of his ideas looking for a visible home in a world he intimately understands. His work is articulated with extreme precision, formulated on canvas within a strict drawing grid. Having seen his preparatory sketches in his studio, I'd say his paintings are architectonic in design, planned and executed with compulsive attention to structure and the relationship between things.

193

The trouble with thinking you're in a Colville painting, as I'm doing, is that it requires you to think about what has always made his work special. And that is the conflicting elements in the composition, the forces that co-exist in quiet or ambiguous tension, inviting you to consider the complex relationships within the picture frame.

So I consider what those conflicting elements could be:

Option one: we have two men, me and Alex, paired by commitment to similar but not identical creative professions, in opposition to our more nurturing, family-oriented partners, our wives, who, understandably, may find aspects of our life mission tiring, or narcissistic at times. Alex and I are friends, not exceptionally close friends, but we're alike in that we've both built practices—his more advanced than mine at this stage—far from the hubs of power in our respective fields, finding inspiration here where, an urbanite might say, there's really nothing to look at.

Option two: we have four people out for a stroll– each of us subject to the indignities of age and time—situated in a spectacular part of the natural world that somehow feels ageless, beyond human time.

Option three: We also have a confrontation here of the present tense with the history beneath our feet, the foundations of a lost village by the sea with a pedigree of cultivation going back thousands of years. Our conversation, intermittent as it is, spins around speculations about what was here so long ago. Where was the garden? The barns? Where did they bury their dead? Dig their wells?

Option four: then I realize, and it's a realization that has been waiting to surface in me since I first met Alex while serving on an art jury with him a few years back, that the elements in conflict—or in tension—in this picture are me, as the architect, and Alex, as the artist.

So much in Alex's work points to a dark view of humanity, his existential doubts about human goodness, likely related to his experience as a young, impressionable war artist in the Second World War. He painted depravity at Bergen-Belsen amid thousands of the dead and dying. A Colville painting isn't a safe journey into rural nostalgia. It is often created from the perspective that the world is a dangerous place, unpredictable, fraught with paradox and, at times, evil. It's too much to say the war ruined him. But his adult children will say, years later, that he suffered nightmares about the war until the end of his life.

There's room for a dystopian or pessimistic sensibility in art. The manifestation of an artist's truth, no matter how dark, is a gift to the world when given by an artist of the first rank, like Alex is. As an architect, I'm necessarily in the optimism business. How can I make the world a better place? By no means is my sensibility completely at odds with Alex's. It's more like we're two sides of the same coin.

"Look," he says. "The daffodils coming up. Isn't that something."

"That's where the flower garden was, the front yard," I say, referring to the foundation nearly overgrown now with brush.

He thinks about that for a long minute, and I can feel him drifting back in time with me to a completely different world.

"Alex, if you breathe deeply enough, I bet you can smell the laundry on the clothesline here two hundred years ago."

Then, a smile on his face. Mischief in it. The man likes to play the part of the small-town hardass: the military brush cut, the reserved manner, the small-c conservative cranky at urban liberals, an artist who wears a lab coat to paint on a schedule as regular as the clock itself, as if he were a scientist of the psyche not just any undisciplined poet, let's say. But there's so much more underneath all that ascetic bluster.

"I have an idea," he says, nodding at our partners behind us.

"Let's pick four daffodils, one for each of us."

A romantic, too.

And so we pick daffodils.

Alex taught me that you can thrive by staying put, settling in one place, settling deep, because it takes a long time, he once told me, to understand how things really work and you can't do that by running around. I take inspiration from his study of the local and domestically familiar, or in my field, the vernacular. How timeless principles can be excavated from what others would consider pedestrian, or ordinary. I like his posture of indifference to his critics. I like his embrace of family life, not finding in it limitation or compromise but the energy and love to prosper as a creative force. I admire his dedication and focus, and that he never quit on anything, despite the odds against him.

The Humanist: Charles Moore

I'm emerging from a dream, the darkness eroding as the wind attacks the bay window and the waves outside pound into the gorge below. As I turn toward these concussive forces, eyes finally blinking open, I detect an internal element in the sonic mix. Across the room, in his sleeping loft, is my boss, among the most famous architects in the world, the intellectual giant who had once worked with Kahn but then rejected Modernist purity by giving voice to postmodernist ideas in our field: Charles Moore. He's snoring up an orchestral storm, each honking sequence spaced by intervals of unbreathing silence that go on too long, as if he's a sputtering engine.

I'm in a sleeping bag stretched out across the built-in benches along the bay window that projects out from his condominium unit, famously known as Unit 9, which sits close to the cliffs. The window allows me to visually fly out over the daunting Pacific while feeling protected inside. This little alcove is a motif that really lives up to Charles' belief that architecture, at its best, scales to our perceptual and emotional capabilities as humans, the idea that we measure and order the world out from our bodies.

As Charles' snoring shows no sign of abating, I slip outside into the bracing air for a run along the bluff trail that winds through meadows separated by belts of Monterey cypress and engulfed at times by roving gusts of fog. I'm accompanied by squadrons of sea birds and the deer that high tail it into the woods when they see me. Breathing harder by the minute, I'm enveloped in the scent of wild iris, one among some five hundred species of native flora here. Coming in and out of view, always, is the Pacific, which today offers up the sleek profiles of porpoises glinting in the morning light and seals sunning in rocky coves. It all makes me homesick for Nova Scotia, a feeling that surprises me in its intensity. This is a world of awesome vistas, a brutal natural beauty that, even after being denuded of its forests of redwood and bishop pine more than a century ago, still feels untouched and untamed. Now it's home to Sea Ranch, the iconic "second-home" community started in the 60s by a group invested in the values of West Coast counterculture: a connection to nature, respect for the environment through active stewardship, the merits of communal living, the need for retreat from the stresses of urban life and consumer culture.

Some ten miles long and a mile wide, Sea Ranch is four thousand acres along the Pacific coast, two hours north of San Francisco. It's home to one of Charles' best works, Condominium One, the place I'm living in right now, which he designed in collaboration with his partners in the MLTW practice and the landscape architect Larry Halprin.

In the design of Condominium One, Moore, as usual, was the so-called thought leader, the lead architect with a vision and the ability to communicate it. But it was through his collaboration with Bill Turnbull, the MLTW partner and architectural craftsman par excellence, that Charles achieved something too often missing in his later work. I learned from them that a good architect—or good architecture, rather—needs to balance vision with craft. It's never either-or. Always so hard to achieve.

In the final stretch of my run, Condominium One comes into view as a kind of natural extrusion in the landscape, a gangly post-and-beam composition cantilevering out of the bluff toward the cliffs, a structure with pitched shed roofs, rough redwood cladding, skylights, and windows punched into the skin pretty much everywhere, bringing in light from all angles. There's a central mass for the shared service elements, around which ten 24-foot cubes—the condo units, including Unit 9—hang saddlebag-style. It's a palace of barn and shed forms, inspired to some degree by local vernacular buildings, all clustered together as if circling the domestic wagons, some elements squeezing up into towers, others burrowing into the cliff, everything stitched together by courtyards, pathways and privacy fences. All units have ocean views, no notable class hierarchy there. As a unified whole, Condominium One, in its efficient yet poetic density, in its respect for the landscape around it, is a landmark in the environmental and sustainable design movement, and really one of the first condominium developments anywhere.

On a property like Sea Ranch, with so much acreage, you'd think there'd be no need for density or any simulation of an urban village. Why not spread out the units, give everyone their own fiefdom? The point was: create a community of the progressively like-minded, everyone huddling together with shared purpose so that the land would not be carved up or degraded into lot-sized slices, but left intact, some of it held in common, a resource to be shared and enjoyed by all. An old-fashioned idea that made sense in old-fashioned agrarian communities where common land had practical jobs to do—pasture animals, provide berry-picking and hunting grounds, store fishing or farming equipment. And here? The land held in common serves a more meditative or quasi-spiritual purpose: appreciation of the land for its own sake. Call it, in an idealistic sense, hippie pantheism. Where the landscape is the god to be served, and where the architecture flowering up in temple-like forms allows the serving of it. That's how Sea Ranch got started, although some twenty years later, the utopian dream has arguably lost a little steam.

The problems started with a ten-year building moratorium imposed by the California authorities when inland residents and eco-activists objected to the Sea Ranch master plan that significantly limited coastline access to folks not owners or tenants on the property. I guess the visionaries of counterculture egalitarianism had blind spots in their definition of communal utopia. But who could blame the developers behind the project for selling ownership on the merits of exclusivity and privacy? As a consequence of the moratorium, the developers were losing money in not being able to build and sell. Eventually, more avenues to the coastline were opened to the public and the moratorium lifted, and money started to flow. Lots were divided up and sold, meadows shrunk, mansions began to sprout, and the architectural fabric of Sea Ranch became more diverse—not always in a good way—as new homeowners hired their own architects in staking their claims as Sea Ranchers. There are a thousand or more homes here today.

198

Politics aside, that Sea Ranch exists at all today is a miracle. What I like most about Condominium One, in the weathering of its form, is its serene impermanence. It's here, for now, for the dreams of the people who built it, holding its own in advance of an inevitable decay. The land will be here in a million years. Not this. Even though the Sea Ranch dream is diminished like so many naively beautiful counterculture ideals, this building has all the power of a mythic ruin in the making.

Back inside, the aroma of fresh coffee. Time for work. And standing at the dining room table, there's Charles, in his bathrobe, hunched over the drawings that I left out last night for a design competition for an art gallery extension. A tall man, heavier than he should be, older-looking than his fifties, he's stooped in the way of someone who constantly struggles to fit his body into a world designed for shorter and slimmer people. But when he hunches at you, it's to connect with you, gently, and empathetically, I'd like to think, coming down to your level or over to your side of things, not just physically, but emotionally, intellectually.

"You sleep well last night, Brian?" Not looking at me.

"Like a log. Hanging out over the cliff like that. Nothing like it."

As his employee this summer, I'm living with him here where I'm working my tail off on a design scheme based on a classic Japanese barn. I'm hopeful he'll appreciate the concept, especially given that as a leading voice in postmodernist thought he's partial to historical precedent. What inspired me to summon the barn, in part, was the time I spent with Charles in Japan, a while back, where we'd been introduced by Larry Richards, the Dalhousie professor who once talked me out of quitting architecture school because of how disappointed I'd been in the educational experience.

In silence Charles and I sit across from one another as he studies my work. I start sketching on another project, keeping busy. This goes on for a while, not a word between us, which is all normal with Charles, as I know well from prior experience. On that trip to Japan, where I had been continuing my studies, I had the opportunity to travel around the country with him to visit architectural and cultural sites. We could go for days without saying much if anything to one another. I'm comfortable with that: words are only a partial and maybe not the most important part of the communication between people. With Charles, I've found he exudes collegiality with his mouth open or shut.

As I wait for him to pronounce on the work, I drift off to a memory I'll always treasure about Japan. Charles and I were visiting Noguchi's home studio, now a museum, a 650-year-old building once lived in by a samurai warrior. And there, among the finished and unfinished sculptures, in the serene simplicity of the interior space, was the perfect Japanese bath. I thought it was the best room in the world. So calm, so considered, yet alive with the rituals and forms of a culture that cherishes the spiritual in constructing space. The bath itself was essentially a wooden stall, surrounded by a floor built with polished river stones, softly illuminated by a slot-window cut into the bottom of a wall, the only light source in the room. You could easily imagine gleaming footprints on those stones, steaming wet from a hot bath. If a room could be both ascetic and sensual at the same time, this was it.

"So, Brian," Charles says, laying tracing paper over my sketches, exhaling audibly now. Here it comes.

First, he looks over to the bay window in the alcove, a lingering glance, then back to me. "When it's time to die, I want to be taken by a giant wave coming in that bay window."

I've heard those lines before, usually after a few drinks. I never tire of its sincerity. Here, in the moment, it's how he softens the blow, as he now carefully traces out the form of my scheme, then proceeds, slowly, to erase most of it, the roof, the columns, leaving mainly a fountain.

"I like the barn idea...but not on this project." So gentle yet so firm.

As crushing as that should sound to me—I'm pretty green, only a year or so out of graduate school—I don't feel erased, not totally, just enough that's good for me. Then I feel included as a new scheme emerges over the fading ghost of mine. Charles knows exactly how to let me down without causing harm, just a little ego bruise that will be gone tomorrow. He's widely known as a master of collaborative design, a process he's labeled *participatory design*. It involves intense interactions and workshops—even some delicately "managed" conflict—with all stakeholders in designing a project, a concept he picked up from the Italian architect and anarchist Giancarlo De Carlo, who was also a mentor of mine when I studied in Sienna. De Carlo, famously, was the founder of ILAUD (International Laboratory of Architecture and Urban Design), a loose international consortium of architects, thinkers and artists, which in some respects provided the model for Ghost.

As diplomatically gentle as Charles is this morning, there's nonetheless an imposition of will going on.

"So what do you think, Brian? Not bad, huh."

"It's got something," I concede, but truthfully uncertain. He'll take uncertainty as a nudge toward agreement.

"It's got something," I repeat, this time with conviction. "Energy."

"What are buildings if not receptacles for human energy? And when they receive enough from us, they give back, too."

He suddenly reconstitutes himself as a man on his feet and announces that it's time for his bath, where the plan isn't just ritual purification but thinking through a thorny problem for his next book. "You take it from here, Brian. You've got it, okay. I like your sense of where it needs to go. And we'll hit the pool for a swim, say about two?"

With Charles, you feel like a valued member of an orchestra he's conducting. In everything I've seen so far he knows how to motivate and empower people and get work done, pollinating situations just enough. Delegation and multi-tasking are part of his genius. Even now, as inexperienced as I am, I see a model here potentially to grow into becoming a more complete architect, like Charles is today, an architect who does big projects, a respected teacher, a thought leader capable of changing the discourse in the field, and a developer, too, a serial builder and seller of homes, including several of his own.

"How about dinner tonight up in Gulala?" he announces from the bathroom. He names a seafood restaurant a half hour up the road.

"A bit of a tourist trap."

"We're all tourists, Brian, remember that." Pleasant but scolding.

Charles has a way of hammering at the ideologue in me that, truth be told, still looks down too critically on mainstream or populist taste as a degrading factor in the built environment. He loves kitsch to a fault I'll say. He's a professional tourist himself, traveling the world as a humble student of architecture to see the master works and vernacular forms across so many cultures, and with his photographic memory, everything turns up in his books, lectures, and conversations with a drink in hand.

Unit 9, the unit he designed for himself, is a shrine to his eclectic interests, with tchotchkes as diverse as a fragment of a Spanish ceiling from Hearst Castle, clay pigs from Oaxaca, a round Baroque mirror, papier-mâché ponies and a toy collection, too. As a loft with exposed beams everywhere, Unit 9 has a precedent of the house he built in Orinda, California, a little wooden hut at heart, suggestive of a Mayan temple or Kahn's bath house in Trenton. The use of aediculae at Orinda—two four-postered "houses within the house"—mirroring how the Greeks and Romans inserted small temples within larger ones—organizes the free-plan at Orinda that includes corner windows that seem to dissolve, allowing nature and the world in. In Unit 9, and in other units here, aediculae are deployed within many of the loft interiors to invest the grids of domestic intimacy with some formal drama.

By early afternoon, our work done for the day, the sun blazing hot, we're in the pool at the athletic club, a short walk away, an ingenious structure dug into a meadow, surrounded by earth berms and trees planted to keep the wind out. We're having a California summer moment. I'm doing laps, pushing myself hard while Charles just floats around, pretending to be disgusted by my desire to stay fit.

"So puritanical." he says. "Yeesh."

Yeesh. An echo of the nerdy kid from rural Michigan.

The man likes to have fun, understanding joy as an essential human experience that architecture needs to stimulate in us, as opposed to, in his view, the humorless severity of late-stage Modernism. When we visited an ancient temple in Kyoto, everything around us so still and solemn, Charles suddenly kicked off his shoes and socks and started dancing and hopping around the moss garden that I'm sure hadn't seen a bare foot in a millennium. Clearly breaking all the rules.

Wheeeeee!

He took me to Disneyland once and we went together on the Pirates of the Caribbean water ride, splashing through a funhouse of glitzy aquatic terrors.

Wheeeeee!

He has tried to convince me that, as motif, Disneyland is an epic garden in the tradition of the sacred grove. I didn't bite. I can't tell at times whether he's serious or pulling my leg, given to citing an extreme example to make a continuing point about how architects in their training dismiss classic forms reborn in the language of popular culture. My gut tells me that the subversive posture of postmodernism, particularly its attachment to historical pastiche, will not benefit Charles' reputation. That his rejection of Kahnian seriousness will have consequences. He knows I feel that way but it doesn't bother him in the least. The few times I've pushed my case—albeit as a respectful irritant—he's given me a look, or a word, as if to say, you go pound a little more sand, there, young man, before telling me what to do.

A kid reminding him of his better self.

I remember Essy telling me—on the matter of Kahnian seriousness—that on Charles' death bed, he'd likely say, pour me another drink. And Kahn, on his, would say, pass me the fucking pencil.

Yeesh.

202

After dinner at Gulala we end up at Larry and Anna Halprin's house at Sea Ranch, on their deck, a peaceful night, where we'll drink into the evening. I listen to Charles, Larry, and Don Lyndon and Bill Turnbull—two of Charles partners in MLTW—tell war stories about building Sea Ranch. At one point, Anna, a dancer and choreographer now in her later sixties, petite, the classic Jewish grandmother, is out on the edge of the deck, dancing away, unconcerned about the lack of a railing to protect her from a terrifying fall to the rocks below.

After too many drinks, we're finally back at Unit 9 to call it a day and soon Charles is upstairs in his loft, snoring blissfully again while I settle again into my sleeping bag in the corner bay window.

As I drift towards sleep, I tell myself that Sea Ranch is a dream about humanism. Charles is a true humanist in the sense that he believes architecture isn't a cult that belongs to the high priests of theory, but to everyone. That everyone, if they care enough, can make a home to suit their lives and dreams.

203

The Partner: Marilyn MacKay-Lyons

Eyes of seawater green—alert yet calm. A striking feature in a striking face softened by long dark hair down to her shoulders.

And long legs.

Longer tonight because of the high-waisted bomber jacket.

That's why I'm staring at my shoes, blushing beet red.

I'm eighteen, she's a year younger. Her bloodline is Scottish DNA but she could pass for Indigenous or Mediterranean. Italian, maybe. The *Love Story* actress Ali McGraw is what I'm thinking. That's a teenaged male in 1972 for you.

Let's step back an hour—

I'm supposed to be the family ambassador, having arrived at the village inn tonight to meet Marilyn and her siblings who are in town with their parents on a vacation trip through Nova Scotia.

My mission, which I grudgingly accepted, is to bring them back to our house for drinks after dinner while the parents go out on the town.

I blow the assignment by sitting aimlessly at the bar as if it isn't obvious who they are, all having dinner at the table in the corner, four young women and two young men who for some reason I think are boyfriends. Now and then I glance over at them, as the tall guy with the varsity smile fusses around her, filling her water glass, passing the rolls and butter, helping her decode the menu.

Yeah, those jocks, they have all the luck.

Until he looms over me, thrusting his big hand into mine.

"You must be, Brian." Turns out he's the older brother, courteous to a fault. He introduces me around the table.

I smile in the right places as I join them for desert.

It's fully clear now that Marilyn and I are being set up.

Earlier I'd heard my mother on the phone, conspiring with Marilyn's mother. Nothing's said or suggested at the table that I'm there to be evaluated for boyfriend suitability but that's the sense I have. Not that Marilyn's openly complicit, as she mentions she has a boyfriend back home. But like me, she's going along for the ride. I don't know how it happens but in the conversation it's revealed in some detail, not by Marilyn, that she's a gifted student and athlete.

Later on I'll learn that her father, Stew, was the real matchmaker in the shadows. Apparently, he recalled meeting me as a boy, a wonderful lad in his recollection, when he and my father were at a business conference down south and the rest of our family tagged along.

An hour later, it appears I'm not deemed an existential threat to Marilyn or her siblings and so we pile into two vehicles and head to our house where I'm expected to be the host until our parents return.

Our house is a trip through Nova Scotia's history. Built on a strategic bend in the Chebogue River in the village of Arcadia near the southern tip of the province, on land where the Mi'kmaq once settled and controlled trade, the house is basically an overwrought collage. One element is a tiny two-room stone structure built, apparently, by Charles LaTour, the French governor of Acadia in the early 1600s, and an ancestor in my family tree. Another element is a Cape Cod brought here disassembled in the 1750s from Nantucket. Paul Revere once spent the night in it, so they say. The final part is half a Cape Cod floated here from what was then called New Amsterdam by a Loyalist fleeing the American Revolution. Since then the place has been renovated half a dozen times. In its charmingly ugly way, this is now our family home, complete with the brown-paneled, early 70s rec room in the basement with the classic Naugahyde bar.

We descend into the basement on a steep narrow staircase, me leading the way, Marilyn right behind. We're being chaperoned, her older brother there with us, along with the rest of the gang. When I switch on the lights, we're confronted by my father's glitzy drum kit, a stuffed crocodile, a medley of Lava lamps, and plenty of other kitsch.

"Would you like to see my Dad's sword collection?"

"Pardon," she says.

I know it's lame before the words are out of my mouth but, as anyone who's ever been in a car crash knows, there are some things you'd like to stop from happening, but they happen anyway, except in slow motion. She looks at me plainly, likely wondering whether if I can make a silk purse out of what is obviously a sow's ear.

So I bring out the weapons, the Nazi dagger, the Borneo headhunter sword, the antique supposedly used in the Charge of the Light Brigade, the two-handed Claymore.

I'm talking each one up like a curator.

"My father collects too," she says brightly.

"He does?"

"He collects bells."

Bells?

"Symbols of peace, Brian. They're often a gift that countries give to each another. Like a diplomatic gesture. But they mean so much more. In Buddhism, they represent *inner peace*."

I have a headhunter's sword in my hands, and it suddenly doesn't feel right. Now I'm hanging out there on a teenaged ledge of anxiety, worried that I've offended her by talking up my father's collection of historical killing artifacts. I'm leaving the wrong impression, because frankly these swords, anything to do with war, isn't my thing at all.

Right now I feel like falling on my sword, actually.

She takes the sword from me, turns it around in her hands, appraising it, eyeing me with those seawater green eyes.

"Some things need to be handled *very* carefully," she says.

She briefly gives it a flourishing turn, as if playing at warrior-queen. Hands it back to me, gingerly, as if dispensing with the corpse of a rat, then, "Brian, you'll have to see my Dad's bell collection."

Flirting. She's playing along with her father's machinations...but compliance here is strictly on her terms. I feel a strange bond, how we're both dutifully but enjoyably inside the roles assigned to us by

205

our parents. How often does that happen these days?

It kind of makes sense. We're both from small-town families and self-made people. We've both been privileged by parents who exposed us to the arts growing up. A lot in common from the get-go.

We still joke about how our marriage was arranged.

I'm still vulnerable to the power of that inner peace of hers, a mix of quiet fearlessness and gentle poise that gives our partnership its enduring vitality and strength.

206

7
SkyRoom III

AFTER SEVERAL DAYS OF FOG AND RAIN, the climate gods are merciful in clearing the air and providing a tentative preview of summer.

The late afternoon sun comes in and out of a restless grouping of clouds as I walk down into Shobac to join Brian's family for a barbecue.

Tonight it's lamb burgers from their flock.

He greets me at the Schoolhouse and suggests we first head over to check out a new house in the area he calls the fishing port. He says that's where we'll find the key that brings everything together at Shobac.

"The key? No better hint than that?"

"Better *show* than *tell.*"

The walk over there along the mud-puddled gravel road feels infected with more drama than in the days before the arrival of that new house, which is a trio of single-story gabled pavilions, Corten clad, built for an American couple. In theory, the Smith House is a home. It has two bedrooms and living spaces consistent with domestic life. But the closer we get, it's clear the place demands to be interpreted as a temple, anchored proudly on a massive granite plinth. It all makes me feel like I've embarked on a *procession*, the kind of journey that shifts your perception of what the moment needs from you.

The Smith House adds heft to a poetic ensemble of urban density. Each of the nine buildings at the fishing port takes cues from the others in the delicate enterprise of village-building. As crowded as things are, the positioning of the buildings gives everyone sufficient visual and sonic privacy. Nothing looks squished. It feels civilized, neighborly. A few buildings were built on slender concrete fins, not foundations, allowing water from tidal surges to flow underneath in bad storms.

The organizing principle here is inspired by the *tartan grid* found in Louis Kahn's design of the Kimbell museum, a touchstone of unsurpassed excellence in High Modern architecture in Brian's estimation. A tartan is, as most of us likely know, a patterned cloth of repeating horizontal and vertical bands of alternating sizes, known most famously as the weave and colors in Scottish kilts. At the Kimbell, the tartan grid features vault-like art galleries of equal size alternating with in-between smaller spaces, all of equal size, for the functional systems and storage. In the fishing port at Shobac, the concept comes alive in a sequencing logic and proportioning of the buildings, and the spaces between them, that speak like musical notes of different time values on a staff. Some buildings and spaces are wider, others narrower, but all relate in their proportions to one another as if they're part of one chain, or rhythmic structure. It's both orderly and dynamic. It's math as music, syncopating the experience as you walk along. You sense an unfolding of elements that are poetically related, not unplanned chaos.

My long-gone parents who came from Acadian fishing villages on Prince Edward Island would have looked at me funny had I told them this place was inspired by a fishing village. But I believe that, if gently led or tutored, they would have eventually connected the design concepts in play with what people built where they grew up.

I'm drawn to the fishing port more than any other area of Shobac probably because the best parts of my childhood were summer vacations in my mother's fishing village. It was total freedom, billeted as I was with my grandparents, away from my parents, outdoors all day, swimming at the beach, fishing smelts at the wharf, shelling poached lobsters delivered to our door in the middle of the night by my uncles. I ran wild in the fields, gleefully firing my pellet gun at squirrels but mostly at my cousins who returned fire equally gleefully. I didn't care if none of my relatives had indoor plumbing or toilets. The experience was an invigorating experience relative to life on the treeless streets of my working-class youth in Montreal.

"As orchestrated as the fishing port is," Brian says, "there's improvisation too. We started with one building, then another, then another. It's like being in a band, where you play to a larger idea, where what comes next depends on what came before, a new idea or variation that brings someone or some other nuance into the story. And here, that variation was what the clients of each of these houses needed or wanted, which determined what we actually built in the grid."

He shakes his head, as if taken aback by something, then says in a self-admonishing voice, "I don't know what I was thinking, building all these houses in one burst over a couple of years, more or less. But first working my tail off to convince people to live cheek-by-jowl like this."

212

There's a lot of money in these houses. Each of the owners could have purchased much larger and more private estates for what they've invested here. But Brian got them all to buy in. My guess is that the compressed period in which all the building took place gives the fishing port a freshness—an energy, maybe—it might otherwise lack with too much premeditation. Some of the best paintings of the world—certainly in the past century—have that quality of freshness that comes from what appears to be improvised gestures. This is not to say that these gestures came without years of prior thoughtfulness or expert training. Still, all the thoughtfulness in the world means nothing without knowing when or how to act in the uncertainty of the moment.

"It was manic," he continues. "Like it was a life-or-death choice. I had to build this place. And now that it's here, honestly, I'm not really sure how it happened. Or whether I could even do it again."

We arrive at a granite retaining wall on our right that runs parallel to the road, the back end of the Smith House plinth. Elevated there behind the wall is the smallest of the three pavilions, the shed, a cozy guesthouse in Corten with bare wood studs inside.

"That little shed, it just sits there on the granite, as poised and yet dynamic, like, a bird on a wire, you might say," Brian says.

Near the shed to our immediate right, looking towards the estuary, we have a view of the back end of the two narrow pavilions of the main residence, which are connected by an eight-foot-wide granite staircase that slides up between the buildings, fusing them as one form.

We turn into the courtyard cut into the granite plinth. There's granite everywhere. It built the grand staircase and the foundation-plinth below the pavilions. The effect of all that granite is to turn Smith House into its own village within the larger fishing port within the even larger village, Shobac. Everything is connected here in conceptual and material lockstep.

I find myself thinking of a morning in Athens long ago, just after sunrise, when I leisurely strolled up the winding road toward the Propylaea, the ceremonial gateway and staircase into the Acropolis. Half of me now is gone to the marble weightiness of those temples in the Greek past and the other half to an unknown future that the Smith House in its granite presumption also seems to be communing with.

The two pavilions of the main residence are staggered in alignment to one another. The "night" pavilion, a bedroom and ensuite, hangs back closer to the road while the mostly glazed "day" pavilion—with the kitchen and great room—slides forward toward the water. In tandem they are two long gabled boxes sliding past one another—an homage to Murcutt's Marie Short House—overlapping for a stretch, creating a Corten-walled channel between them. And that's where we find ourselves, going up the staircase between the buildings and into breathtaking water views.

The day pavilion is constructed with black steel trusses visible inside. Windows everywhere. Sliding metal screens on the windows control light flow and maintain privacy. Triple-glazed doors and window vents provide cross-ventilation. The high ceilings are warmly textured in white ash veneer. Anchoring everything is a five-ton granite mantle over the fireplace in the great room. Because there is so much glass curtain wall, it looks like the stone hearth is holding up the entire building.

When we step inside, I'm drawn forward with divining-rod eagerness to a glass wall cantilevered over the foundation, facing the water. The views, capped at a seven-foot height, take most of the sky out of the scene, emphasizing the sea-level vista, the ultimate infinity pool. It's a room designed for prospect, for surveying the world.

Next door, the night pavilion, is sunken a few feet below the granite plinth surface: a serene chapel, womb-like, a cave. Designed for refuge, nocturnal calm, slowness, privacy.

Prospect and refuge are the twinned attributes of experience these structures aspire to, as they do in all of Brian's best work.

Below the plinth, on one edge of the property, is a granite wall made from small boulders of irregular dimensions, all packed in together. "It's an old-fashioned sheep wall," Brian says. "It's the kind of rough boundary the earliest settlers could build without having to carve up stone. It's a contrast we wanted with the rectilinear grid over most of the plinth, as if to say, this is a building that goes very far back in time."

The sheep wall is a tough-looking but beautiful mosaic. When seen from a distance across the flat green field that it borders, the sheep wall conveys the impression that it's been here forever.

"In so many agrarian cultures, you'd wake up in the morning and open the shutters, and the sheep would be there to start your day," Brian says. "And that's what happens here some days."

The question nagging me is this: if the Smith house is a temple, what's it worshipping?

It doesn't assert a hierarchy of gods from the conventional lexicon of spirituality, or render fables about the articles of faith, unlike stained-glass narratives or Classical pedimental sculpture. To my eyes, as an apparition in the landscape, the Smith House performs an alchemic function as a medium for mystical experience. By mystical I mean what's common to most of us: how the natural beauty of the world can make you wonder in astonishment about how it all came to be. Obviously, Nature-as God is hardly a new manifestation of the spirituality impulse. Maybe a less sentimental way of putting it is that Brian's buildings at Shobac invite you to look intensely at everything around them, thus seeing the landscape as the real story. It's like the buildings are saying, our effect is rooted in the landscape that we cultivate by our presence and for your benefit. We channel forces in the landscape, not just sit in it. Our beauty is a proxy for universal beauty.

With all that granite and iron in its bones—the stuff mined from the geological marrow of this rugged landscape—the Smith House is built for a much longer lifespan than a fishing shack made of wood and raised on stilts over the tidal violence of the sea. Of all the buildings Brian has built here, this is the first risen on the illusion that you can build something to last centuries. It's not implausible that in three or four hundred years something of the Smith house will still be here, if the spit is still here, which is fragile ecologically, continuously shape-shifting as all coastlines do. If the spit is no longer here, some part of the house will likely still be here—underwater, perhaps—unless the barbarians and iconoclasts of the future scavenge it for parts. Even if the disappearance of the Smith House is a long time away, that threat perversely adds to its allure today.

Brian tells me, "Two influences here. One is Taliesen West, where Wright's idea was to build tents over the historic ruins in the landscape. Louis Kahn is the other guy, not just for his tartan grid, but the mystic in him especially. His master works present themselves as heaviness, or mass, in service to light. He was interested in the weight of the world we carry around inside us, the gravity of the human situation, even as there's always a part of us trying to escape, to reach beyond our limitations to the deeper mysteries. That's where Kahn as the architect of light comes into play. Light as a medium for spirituality, the passageway or medium to it."

"Yes, but how does that play out here?"

"What could be more mysterious and larger than nature, the landscape, the sea and the sky all around us and—"

He stops himself, shakes his head again, as if undone by internal debate, then: "Kahn's boots are big ones to fill. And here I am, in a little fishing village in Nova Scotia. I have people telling me, Brian, you build shacks on *stilts*, no foundations, in wood. Boats that sail on the land. And now this? Stone, steel, weight. Temples. Are you losing it?"

"Well, what are you doing?"

"There's iron in the headlands here, Gaff Point, Rose Head, Hell Point. Granite too. Millions and millions of tons all over the landscape, left behind by the glaciers. So in a way, I am reaching into the past, to the deepest story in the landscape, to iron and granite. I guess on some level I'm building new ruins to keep the old ruins company."

Once we're outside again on the granite plinth, in a rectangular courtyard framed by the pavilions, we have views across the valley to where we came from. Messenger House II sits proudly on the drumlin ridge in the distance, a guardian presence on the landscape that mariners easily can pick out from offshore. The hillside pastures below it, all around the valley, are thickly pinpricked in sheep. Off in their own field are the Highland cattle. Long-haired, big-horned beasts.

"Now what about that key you mentioned, Brian?"

"Look *down*, think what you're standing on, right now. And also think what you were looking at, near the Studio, straight ahead."

The clues eventually reveal the story: the rectangular granite courtyard I'm standing on relates, in its dimensions and location in the valley, to the old foundation, the SkyRoom, visible here directly across the fields near the Studio. The foundation over there, Brian now tells me, is something akin to the mold for the plinth over here. That would make the granite here the missing internal content of the SkyRoom. The Skyroom is the lock interior. The Smith plinth is the key that fits it.

In belly button parlance: one's an innie, the other an outie.

"And that's the key I'm talking about," he says. "The fusing of here and there. The idea that everything at Shobac—in all my work—flows or relates backs to the SkyRoom. Unifying everything."

"Well, the foundation connects you to the past, obviously."

"It's more than a passage through time, but a connection to *each other*. Let's say you're standing here, as you are now, looking across the field to the SkyRoom, where I or Marilyn might be sitting. We would both know we're in the same room."

"The same room in two places."

"A shared perception of place, if not the same room physically, but on a deeper level that all good neighbors intuitively understand."

He steps away to take a call, giving me time alone to think about all this as the setting sun lavishes Shobac in a sympathetic glow, every building getting its celebrity turn in the dying light.

If we take on faith that the plinth and foundation are one room in two places, we have to reckon with the properties of the space between them. We would have to believe the space across the field isn't empty of meaning but creates it. In Brian's scheme it's a conduit for our wiring as humans, our need for connection. Of course, architects of quality have always thought about how buildings and the spaces inside and between them connect us. But sometimes you need to be shown, or reminded, how it works to affirm what you intuitively know, or what you should know. Right now it's invigorating, as I wait for Brian's return, to stare across the valley toward the SkyRoom, standing on the plinth, breathing in the heavy coastal air, squinting through shifting layers of daylight.

I really do feel, myself, for the moment, that I exist in two places.

All the buildings at Shobac, much like the fishing port except on a larger scale, are in visible proximity to one another, not cloistered on their own behind walled enclosures and other vigilant guardians of privacy, which is increasingly what we expect when architecture meets the financial means to procure upmarket or corporatized isolation. It's not a kibbutz-style commune here, either. But at Shobac total privacy is foregone as the ultimate luxury in favor of neighborly intimacy.

While Brian has been involved in building other communities from the ground up, the truth is that most of his work over his career, no surprise, has been built in an imperfect world where only a few variables are controlled. Here, for now at least, everything that rises out of the ground is rooted in his vision and his family's resourcefulness. As separate as each building is, the ensemble really works together as one thing, a unified thing, that in this brief moment unifies me.

When Brian returns, I say, "It's really one thing, isn't it?"

"Including the spaces between—the views being framed. It's like the white space in a painting, or the music between the actual notes."

* * *

When we start our walk back to the Studio for the family barbecue, I ask him how the master plan at Shobac evolved.

"We didn't have one."

"Come on. The place looks so...structured, so complete."

"Always complete, but never complete."

"You're losing me."

"I mean each step leads to another. It's like the Laurie Anderson song, *Walking and Falling.* She gets at the essence of forward motion, or locomotion. How we get through life, how we move toward what we think we want, whatever it might be. When you're walking, with each step, and it's not something you always realize, you're also falling a little, at risk, until you catch yourself. Shobac is a little like that, except there have been many times when I barely caught myself. I guess one thing led to another, then to another. Some of the things we first built, the temporary buildings, the early projects, some were not in the right place or not built right, and so we took them down when their time came."

He says *when their time came* as if these departed structures were beloved elders whose passing were an inevitable if tragic part of the natural cycle of things. He sees I'm not convinced about the improvisational plan in creating Shobac as it exists today.

"I'm not great with sports analogies. But I sort of see myself as a quarterback, being chased by a dozen large, angry men. So you zig and zag, not thinking what you're doing...just doing. All based on a lifetime of learning and, yes, hard work. Call it *cultivated intuition.* So you just know what to do. Split-second decisions. And you know the danger of a mistake. We could have never planned Shobac in advance, other than we knew where we could go, if the field opened up. So we zigged, then zagged."

"Can you build a city thinking like this?"

"You think planning in most cities is any good?"

Disgust.

218

"If it all burned down here one night," he says, giving me a pirate-eyed gleam, "I'd be out here the next morning, starting over. Put me on a desert island with a shovel and I'll give you a city."

Suddenly a slash of black movement overhead and a buzzing sound. For a second, I'm wondering if something's gone wrong with my eyes. I soon realize the object is a drone. My next thought is that it's a wayward device from a Coast Guard exercise in the area, until I see Brian's son, Matt, basketball-player lanky, ear-budded, loping along below it on the road, gripping the controller.

Matt's a charmer, laconically funny, brainy, could talk the night into believing it's day, a fan of podcasts on mind-bending stuff, the ethics of AI, the future of carbon-capture, the political situation in Sri Lanka, the history of rap music. Like his siblings, he's signed up to be an integral part of the future at Shobac, and that means being committed to the endless chores that come with stewarding it, building fences, planting gardens, caring for the animals, attending to visitors, holding events. And posting on social media to promote their cottage rental business.

"It's video, for Instagram," he shouts at me.

The video-shooting drone hovers over a pasture, scaring the bejesus out of the sheep that spread to the four corners. Matt does something causing the drone to rise higher. And then backs away up the road, the drone following him, an airborne puppy on a digital leash.

As we continue on, following Matt, we're confronted by a piercing yelp from inside the Troop Barn. An animal in pain, because it isn't human, can't be. The yelps continue, discrete bursts of anguish, then the intervals slowly lengthen, then silence.

"Let's go in for a look," Brian says, heading up the steps, assuming I will follow, while Matt continues on his way.

In the vast space under the cathedral ceiling, one of the family's two dogs, Maudie, a bear-like Leonberger, a mass of brown fur with eyes as large as hockey pucks, lies on a blanket, awake but calm, attended by Brian's daughter, Ali, the veterinarian, who looks at us with her striking blue eyes—her father's eyes—shaded in concern. In her early thirties, she's recently a mum for the second time.

"Dad, I don't think the ligament is fully torn, but it is inflamed so I did some acupuncture on it. She's ok with it."

For years we were accustomed to seeing Ali with her two horses, riding or walking them in the fields or on the beach, always ready to help a wary child reach up and pet her animal companions, or sit on them, like both my sons did so long ago now, it seems.

As we stand around chatting, the dog finally sits up, and comes tail-wagging over to Ali, and is evidently good-to-go for dinner. Then all of us, the limping dog included, head over to the SkyRoom, soon joined by another Leonberger, Lucca, barking madly beside the Schoolhouse.

When we step down into the SkyRoom, Matt is working the grill while scrolling his phone with aplomb and chatting with his fiancé, Abi, a doctor, to whom he recently proposed at Shobac, on bended knee, up on a drumlin ridge overlooking the ocean. Romance? Yeah, Shobac has that too. It isn't all history, landscape and architecture.

Matt's drone is asleep in the corner.

I have an urge to pet it but don't.

In one corner, Ali's husband, Nathan, an engineer, keeps an eye on two-year old Henry, who is quietly assembling a large toy without help, much to the delight of his grandmother, Marilyn, also within hovering distance. She's holding Ali and Nathan's second child, baby Claire.

220

A tall blond woman, mid-thirties, Renée, the structural engineer who recently moved back here with husband Peter, visibly her mother's daughter, all clear green eyes and a warm smile, sets out condiments on a long wooden table. Renée and Peter have just welcomed their first child, Theo, who's being rocked to sleep by Peter up in the Studio.

Renée is navigating her way to me around the dogs, so gentle and sensitive as a general rule, but unrelenting in their slobbering demand for her attention and scraps of human food. Even while doing that, there's a part of Renée's brain dedicated to ensuring I'm being taken care of, that there's a beer in my hand, that my iPhone is charged, and inquiring whether I have any food allergies, dietary restrictions.

Renée, like her siblings, has a well-tuned social intelligence that comes from long experience—doubtless some of it tedious—helping her parents host countless dinners, conferences and parties here over the years, along with meeting the needs of guests renting their cabins.

Like all families, of course, this family has its secrets behind the behavioral protocols established about what they show outsiders and how they negotiate their relationships privately to one another.

Here they are tonight, a genuinely welcoming group, hospitable, happily together in a way that feels deeper than appearances. If it's a performance in family harmony I'm getting, it's convincing. What's clear is their passion for Shobac. It's their home, after all, built over decades with sacrifices they've all made. And now that a village, or community, has risen over the ghosts of forgotten ones, there will be more sacrifices required to keep things whole in this unfolding adventure.

Brian talks about cultural genius trumping individual genius.

Well, family genius will be required here to go forward.

* * *

After the barbecue and cleanup, Brian and I stroll toward the cliffs for a look at another new element in the infrastructure here.

Along the estuary on which Shobac fronts, there's a massive sea wall, built recently with countless tons of granite boulders. This isn't something you build on weekends with a few guys and a case of beer. It's a major investment in the long-term stability of the Shobac valley. And it's money that needed to be spent, given everyone's fears, everywhere, of rising sea levels and extreme weather. In recent years, some storms have eaten more from the cliffs than everyone expected. Whether it's an alarming deviation from the long-term historical norm isn't so easy to answer. Regardless, the erosion has reached a point where something had to be done to protect what's built on the land behind the cliffs.

You can delay the sea in its advances but you can't stop it, not in the long run.

Brian points out that, relative to the open ocean to the south, Shobac is well protected today by the high rock dunes on the beach and the Gaff Point headland. Its longest water-exposed flank, where the seawall was built, fronts on the relatively quieter river estuary. So there's a fair possibility in his view that nothing drastically changes here over the next fifty years, that erosion will not accelerate faster than the incremental shifts historically experienced, even with rising sea levels, and that the seawall will do the job it was constructed to perform.

"That seawall was a *financial bomb* that landed on us," Brian admits. "But it really had to be done. Had to. I mean, every time I see an old barn falling down, uncared for, I see Albert Oxner dying. How do you think I feel looking at the land I've spent twenty-five years of my life clearing, and watching it disappear under my feet?"

* * *

Coastal erosion I'm acquainted with.

My mother grew up on the shores of Prince Edward Island in an Acadian fishing village that has mostly washed away. Years ago the dunes were destroyed once and for all by a series of storms, causing flooding and endangering the houses behind them. As is common on dune beaches, the sand creeps inland over time, trying to avoid the damage, some experts argue, that comes with rising sea levels. And so, eventually, every home near the beach in my mother's village was moved inland.

It's not an uncommon situation on the Island. Unlike Nova Scotia's geology which is largely bedrock—harder stuff in general—the Island is basically one big sandbar, its cliffs made of red sandstone that crumbles away very easily. The Island, I guess, is made to vanish at some point in distant geological time.

Much of my mother's village now exists only as sea glass buried in sand, the fragments of bottles and crockery from the long-gone general store and the local dump. My sister still walks the beach there and as a consequence has amassed a sea-glass collection that numbers several thousand pieces that are bottled up in glass jugs. At times it saddens me that sea glass is all that remains of my mother's world. But I find something uplifting in these often luminous, colorful artifacts, imagining that each piece has a story to tell about the bygone world it came from.

My mother and her relatives lived in houses that were poor relations to the good generics Brian talks about, like the Campbell cottage. After she married my father, who grew up in a neighboring village further inland, they ran away from the poverty by moving to Montreal where they built a modest life and raised my sister and I.

The boyhood summer vacations I spent in my mother's fishing village infected me with whatever virus of the spirit that eventually drew me to the Nova Scotia coast in my thirties and disabled me from ultimately settling anywhere else.

Years ago, when our boys were joyous little creatures, all big eyes and rosy cheeks and high-pitched Martian voices inside their fluffy red hoodies, I brought them to Shobac one day in the fog to see the four cabins under construction (Ghost 7). Both boys were, stereotypically, play-time builders in their sandbox on our land and on the beaches, content for hours building worlds of their own that lasted until the rain fell or the tide came in. At Shobac I watched them clamber all over the skeletons of the cabins, envying their purpose and innocence.

I wonder now if all the summers we spent here as a family will one day awaken a desire in them to spend more time by the sea again, as it did for me when I reached a certain age.

I wonder if the beaches I walk today will still be around for them and their children should they be fortunate enough to have them.

* * *

Brian talks about a room being in two places. There's a part of me that wants and maybe needs to believe there is a second Brian and Marilyn—their doubles—operating in two places at once at Shobac. How they do everything is a mystery to me. They operate the farm pretty much on their own, as they do the tourist business, in addition to conducting busy professional careers in town that take them out of the country at times. They have some hired help but it's almost invisible, a few part-timers who drift in and out, helping with the sheep, the upkeep on the properties, cleaning the rental units. They're formidable in their focus and energy, but they're approaching their mid-sixties. There's obviously a limit to what they can give to Shobac in the years ahead.

Their adult children, and their partners, are now taking on bigger roles here that include being involved in figuring out what happens next at Shobac as a family business.

My own hope is that one day there will be a foundation based here—a social enterprise supported by a diversity of patrons—to preserve and interpret the architectural legacy. Brian's buildings here, including the Ghost projects long gone, are important beyond their presence in the landscape or as a portal for understanding the history here, the heritage that otherwise would remain buried, in ruins. They are valuable as our future heritage.

* * *

So much has been written about Brian with great insight and sensitivity by gifted architectural critics. For this project I learned much from their work that I cannot hope to imitate or match. I have tried to synthesize some of their expert perspectives and, in a modest way, here and there, make my own contributions as an informed amateur who has thought about Brian's work for a long time.

The buildings here are sculptural but they're not art. But like art, they tell a story about their origins and intentions. As story-telling devices, the buildings are sometimes, plainly, metaphors in built form. They invite you to make connections to things easily identified with a little effort: lanterns, sun dials, boats, lighthouses, barns, fishing shacks, temples. Other buildings summon more abstract associations: a knife-form slicing at the sky, a facade that rises up like a cliff face, and box configurations arguing for the beauty of rectilinear simplicity.

What intrigues me the most about Brian's buildings here is how they transcend the moment while being part of it.

224

We all know of new buildings that live mostly in the past. That's nostalgia, sentimentality. Think faux French chateaus in the better neighborhoods.

We all know buildings that point mainly to the future, the latest shiny object created in the techno-utopian spirit of Silicon Valley, where the past and even the present are devalued as inspiration.

And then there are buildings that speak only to the present, unaware of much else. McMansions. The cookie-cutter housing developments, condo towers and malls plopped down in cities and suburbs across the planet that all look and feel the same.

The *bad generic*.

Of course there's great design out there produced by great architects all over the world.

But there's a point being made at Shobac about the qualities we intuitively respond to in architecture—or I respond to. Brian's sensibility as an architect and community builder is a compelling fusion of voices from the past, present and future. In his buildings you experience their time-traveling ambitions, a reach that corresponds to the instincts of the human imagination that also transcends time.

In the ensemble at Shobac, there's a quality of aliveness connecting everything, a forceful blend of the poetic and the pragmatic. It's evident in how some buildings appear to actually move through the landscape, or channel the forces in nature they confront. Weirdly, for all the architecture in the valley, the buildings never upstage the landscape but enhance the experience of it. And like the best art, Brian's buildings at Shobac have something mysterious about them, an indefinable aspect that draws you to see what—or who—is inside them.

The farm aspect of Shobac speaks to an idealized version of the agrarian past. But what is being farmed? Sheep, yes. Seventy or eighty head of sheep meet an operational definition of a flock. But a few Highland Cattle don't make a herd of cattle. And the garden is only big enough to feed one family or perhaps a little more. What's ultimately being farmed here are ideas about architecture and how to build structures and communities worth living in.

If the world turns out right, one day Shobac will be studied in earnest by those interested in the architectural treasures of the world. In the learning environments of our tomorrows, in whatever form they take, I can easily imagine an impressionable student much like I once was, awakened by a message from the past that enriches the present and opens up an inspiring way of walking towards the future.

IMAGE CREDITS

The MacKay-Lyons Family—Brian, Marilyn, Renée, Alison and Matthew—thank you for allowing me into your lives.

Brian & Marilyn—thank you for the inspiration in what you've achieved at Shobac and your trust in me.

Brian—This book is as much yours as it is mine. The time we spent working together I'll always treasure.

Oro Editions—Gordon Goff, Jake Anderson and the publishing team. Professional, imaginative, inspiring. If there is a publishing heaven, you guys are it.

Concrete—As a favor to me, my close friends John Pylypczak and Diti Katona so generously put together and supported an outstanding (and super-talented) design and production team. Thanks to designers Rebecca Wilkinson and Matthew Sabloff, project manager Kelly McLarty and production director Brandy McKinlay. All wonderful to work with.

Sara Angel—for believing in this project and for always being there as a voice of expertise and encouragement.

Andy Wainwright—my friend and compadre in all things literary.

Peter Cavelti—a trusted and insightful first reader, a long-time friend, mentor and inspiration.

Aaron Bourgoin—without whom I wouldn't be writing about architecture or maybe even be interested in it.

Paryse Beatty—for supporting the work in putting together the photography for the book.

"Heir to McLuhan."
—THE NATIONAL POST

"The exact nature of what this estimable writer offers matters less than the fact that he offers it at all—intelligently, vulnerably, often poetically."
—THE GLOBE & MAIL

"A [writer] so laden with vision and ideas and cultural insights and narrative experiment that I fell to the floor and cried for mama."
—QUILL & QUIRE

Larry Gaudet has published seven books: two novels, a family memoir, and four works that blend fiction and non-fiction and, in the end, defy easy categorization. His scriptwriting through his 300 Dead Cattle subsidiary includes projects with Universal Cable, NBC, and various Los Angeles producers that include Highway Bingo and Chernin. His corporate work over 25-plus years spans branding, venture financing, speechwriting, investor relations, and marketing. He has been a partner in a contemporary art gallery. He has received Canada's highest journalism awards and recognition from branding juries internationally. His community work includes providing strategic counsel to Doctors Without Borders (MSF Geneva), the Kingsburg Coastal Conservancy in Nova Scotia, an art therapy institute in Hangzhou, China, and the Art Canada Institute in Toronto. He's a Dalhousie graduate with a diploma from the Canadian Securities Institute. He lives in Canada.

ORO Editions
Publishers of Architecture, Art, and Design
Publisher: Gordon Goff

www.oroeditions.com
info@oroeditions.com

Published by ORO Editions

Managing Editor: Jake Anderson

10 9 8 7 6 5 4 3 2 1 First Edition

ISBN: 978-1-954081-20-8

Color Separations and Printing: ORO Group Ltd.
Printed in China.

ORO Editions makes a continuous effort to minimize the overall carbon
footprint of its publications. As part of this goal, ORO Editions, in association
with Global ReLeaf, arranges to plant trees to replace those used in the
manufacturing of the paper produced for its books. Global ReLeaf is an
international campaign run by American Forests, one of the world's oldest
nonprofit conservation organizations. Global ReLeaf is American Forests'
education and action program that helps individuals, organizations, agencies,
and corporations improve the local and global environment by planting and
caring for trees.